CYPHERS & SIGHS

A High-Stakes Global Thriller of Love, Loyalty and Deceit

By Glen Hellman

Disclaimer: This is a work of fiction. Names, characters, businesses, places, events, locales, and incidents are either the products of the author's imagination or used in a fictitious manner. Any resemblance to actual persons, living or dead, or actual events is purely coincidental.

© 2023 by Glen Hellman. All rights reserved. No part of this publication may be reproduced, distributed, or transmitted in any form or by any means, including photocopying, recording, or other electronic or mechanical methods, without the prior written permission of the publisher, except in the case of brief quotations embodied in critical reviews and certain other noncommercial uses permitted by copyright law.

"Chess is life in miniature. Chess is struggle, chess is battles."

– Garry Kasparov

CYPHERS & SIGHS

Foreword

Where did this book come from? I'll tell you. You see, the author, who is me, will explain its origins, inspirations, and the people who helped me with the book here.

Glen Hellman, that's me, was born in 1955, graduated from JP Stevens High School in Edison, NJ, in 1974 and the University of Maryland in 1978. Upon graduating I joined an early-stage startup, Lexitron, that was acquired by Raytheon. I was one of the early employees of Progress Software, which went public in 1991. I was one of the principals of Call Technologies, where I raised $12 million from top Venture Capitalists before selling the company to 3Com for $100 million cash.

I spent ten years as a hired-gun turn-around executive working for private equity investors on their failing startups. I've been an angel investor and am currently a member of the faculty of the A. James Clarke School of Engineering at the University of Maryland, and an executive Leadership Coach.

Cyphers & Sighs is the fourth addition to my bucket list of creative activities. Now completed, my bucket list includes writing a non-fiction book, Intentional Leadership, available on Amazon, writing and performing a stand-up comedy act, which a competent Googler could find on YouTube, along with several songs written and performed by me. My favorite song, you ask? Why it's "Jersey Cowboy," of course.

Many of the stories in this book are inspired by real people, events, and incidents, including how I landed my first job, hired a global VP of sales in London, and encountered a demented woman who showed up at the Marine Corps Intelligence office, at Henderson Hall, behind the Pentagon.

Many of the people in the book are inspired by but not representative of people who I've worked with or known throughout my life.

The inspiration for this book comes from an unlikely place. Chapter 1, The Woman At The Bar, took place after my sales team completed a meeting in 1989, and we convened at Ditka's bar on Rush Street. I've related the story many times since, and it elicited laughs and an occasional, you should write about that sometime. And so, 35 years later, I finally used it as a device to start a story.

Inspirations for this book are numerous, and I don't want to name them because you may assume they are the characters within. But I must thank two people: Joe Enrico, a great friend of over 40 years who is in the process of writing a literary masterpiece and inspired me to write a less high-brow, dime store novel. Joe was an immense help, suggesting helpful edits and plot twists. I also have to thank my wife, Nancy, who is my Dee; she's just as beautiful and smart, half as devious, and worked diligently to give feedback and copy-edit this book.

I hope you enjoy reading this as much as I enjoyed writing it, and I thank you for getting to this part of my forward. Keep reading.

All the best,
Glen Hellman
November 2023

TABLE OF CONTENT

Foreword 5
Prologue ix
Let the Game Begin 1
Part I - The Pieces on the Board 3
    Chapter 1 - The Woman At The Bar 5
    Chapter 2 - A knock at the door. 11
    Chapter 3 - Unexpected Encounters 19
    Chapter 4 - Home Turmoil. 25
    Chapter 5 - Reunion Across the Pond 29
    Chapter 6 - Strategies and Suspicions 33
    Chapter 7 - Morning Run Revelations. 41
    Chapter 8 - Sales Meeting Showdown. 45
    Chapter 9 - Goodman Canary Wharf Chronicles. 49
Part II - Queen's Pawn to D4 55
    Chapter 10 - The Pot Gets Stirred 57
    Chapter 11 - Cracks in the Facade 65
    Chapter 12 - Bonds of Friendship 69
    Chapter 13 - Meeting Adjourned 73
    Chapter 14 - An Unexpected Evening 75
    Chapter 15 - Unwinding Threads. 79
    Chapter 16 - Unseen Eyes 85
    Chapter 17 - The Games Begin 89
    Chapter 18 - Fight or Flight 95

- Chapter 19 - Plan to Action 103
- Chapter 20 - Layers of Security. 109
- Chapter 21 - Truth Unveiled 113
- Chapter 22 - Everyone Has A Plan Until They're Punched In The Mouth 115
- Chapter 23 - Tokyo Sunrise 119
- Chapter 24 - Tell Me No Secrets 131
- Chapter 25 - Domestic Comfort. 131
- Chapter 26 - Plans and Peace. 135
- Chapter 27 - Transfer Of Power. 139

Part III - Checkmate. 145

- Chapter 28 - Dee's Gift 147
- Chapter 29 - Ripples of Fate 151
- Chapter 30 - Peace and Understanding 157
- Chapter 31 - Memorial. 161
- Chapter 32 - Phoebe. 165

Epilogue. 171
After the End 173
About the Author: Glen Hellman. 177

Prologue

"The hardest thing to do in chess is to do nothing."
— *Garry Kasparov*

LET THE GAME BEGIN

Langley, Virginia

At the CIA headquarters, nestled deep beneath layers of security, the basement computer room hummed with the sound of servers and sophisticated machinery. Here was the silent guardian of national digital intelligence. Bill House, a late shift computer operator of ordinary skills, sat behind a console monitoring routine system traffic. His fingers paused over the keyboard as an anomaly appeared on his screen—a curious cyber intrusion.

Rapid keystrokes resonated in the quiet chamber, punctuating the gravity of the moment. With a series of commands, Bill effectively countered the breach, thwarting the hacker with ease. Still, he thought he should summon Anna Walsh, the agency's top cybersecurity analyst.

As Walsh analyzed the breach's digital signature, a puzzled frown creased her brow. The intrusion pattern was almost too straightforward as if it were meant to be discovered. "It's almost like they wanted us to find it," she murmured to Bill. The immediate threat had been neutralized, but she couldn't shake off the feeling that this was merely a distraction, perhaps a ploy to elicit and test the agency's defenses. The simplicity with which Bill had thwarted the breach wasn't a testament to his skill but rather to the intruder's true intentions.

"We are going to have to monitor this more closely, there is more to this than it seems," she said, and added, "Put a note in your journal that this is likely a precursor to something more virulent. I want us all on a yellow alert status until further notice."

Part I - The Pieces on the Board

"In chess, as in life, a strong beginning sets the stage for all that follows."
— *Anonymous*

CHAPTER I

THE WOMAN AT THE BAR

Ryan Harman, aiCheckmate's Chief Revenue Officer, and his US sales team wrapped up the first day of a two-day National Sales Meeting in Chicago. Contrary to the casual attire standard among software professionals, his sales team is suited up, a preference of Harman's. aiCheckmate is a darling of the tech world, with seventy million dollars in venture funding, and Ryan always believed in the old adage: Dress for success. He would not tolerate any black mock turtleneck, blue-jeaned, Steve Jobs wannabes on his team.

aiCheckmate's initial AI product, Stalemate, was widely recognized as the top cyber-security software product on the market, it harnessed an AI engine to monitor all access points and elements of an organization's systems, then recognized and immediately employed countermeasures to thwart intrusion attempts.

On a cold, damp Chicago October night, the team found themselves at Pippin's Tavern on Rush Street, letting their hair down. Eight of them, five men and three women, settle into the rhythm of the night, raising their glasses and swapping tales, each taller than the last.

"We're celebrating Vanessa's big win. Drinks are on her." Joked Harman as he raised his bourbon glass for a toast. "This deal is going to open a lot of doors for everyone around the table." Vanessa, a tall, handsome young woman, was one of Ryan's top performers. She recently closed an eight-million-dollar deal with a three-letter agency referred to as customer X.

Vanessa Jones was a combination of Einstein and Coco Chanel, a fashionista with an MS in Electrical Engineering from MIT. She was one in a thousand engineers who could speak and relate to humans. Her territory was the District of Columbia, Maryland, and

Virginia, commonly referred to as the DMV, and she worked closely with the Defense and Intelligence agencies.

Ryan met her at an MIT career day five years ago. It took a lot of determination and grit for a woman, especially a Black woman, to graduate with honors from MIT. He wanted her on his team and didn't think he had a prayer of recruiting her, but she accepted his offer despite the fact that Ryan hadn't prayed or stepped into a church since his marriage over a decade ago.

It wasn't the prayer or lack thereof that attracted Vanessa. She had college loans, which thoughts and prayers wouldn't pay off. She was motivated by the money. Ryan offered her the opportunity to work for a well-funded startup unicorn, offering a respectable salary, stock options, and the prospects of the gold and riches in the commissions she'd earn by selling the world's most innovative cyber-security software to the most demanding, well-funded, intelligent agencies in the world.

"So, Vanessa," Chris Long asked, "have you ordered your Gulfstream yet?"

Vanessa responded, "I'm looking at Mercedes money on this deal. The Gulfstream will have to wait till next year, Chris… Chris?" She frowned at Chris, realizing he hadn't heard a word she said. Chris's eyes were laser-focused on a moving target that had just entered the room. The volume in Pipin's seemed to hush as all eyes, male and female, fixated on the exotic, raven-haired beauty who walked across the room to sit at the bar.

Vanessa's win and the group's chatter were put on hold as the team was treated to the live-action version of Swipe Left. One after another, potential suitors walked up to the woman and left in dejection.

Lenny Baxter, aiCheckmate's San Francisco, West Coast rep, suggested they start a pool… Lenny was a heavy-set, jovial, fifty-six-year-old divorcee who had been carrying a bag for Silicon Valley startups since graduating from San Diego State thirty years ago. He suggested a betting pool to see how many men crashed and burned before someone was invited to sit with the woman. Baxter would bet on anything. He once proposed that Ryan and he bet if the next bird to take a crap on a car would be a pigeon or a seagull. Ryan didn't take the bet... by the way, anyone with money on a crow would have won.

As Lenny started explaining the rules of the game, Chris, a twenty-eight-year-old, former TCU tight end, and the newbie to the team, swirled his Blanton's, tipped his hat, donned his best, albeit questionable, John Wayne drawl, and announced, "Reckon I'll head on down the range, make sure that little lady over yonder isn't bothered by any more no-good varmints."

The team giggled and teased and watched as he left the table.

Tall, with a cowboy's stride and sandy hair contrasting with his dark suit and cowboy boots, Chris boldly approached the mysterious beauty.

From their vantage point, the aiCheckmate squad watched with bated breath, trading suppressed chuckles as Chris joined the singed pile of failed suitors. He returned to the table, and Ex-Marine Dexter "Dex" Johnson quipped, "Dang shame how she wounded you, Chris. Do I need to call a medic? Let me check you for a pulse."

Dex was a Naval Academy grad who did his time in Afghanistan. He loved the Corps, his comrades, and the brotherhood. Yet one day, after a particularly trying mission, he calculated he wasn't earning enough dollars per bullet aimed his way. He concluded he could live longer, eat better, and make more dollars per bullet in a career where people weren't aiming to shoot him. Dex joined the aiCheckmate team two years ago, lived in Boston, and his territory was New England. Ryan admired him and respected him. They were both developing a trusted relationship.

Everyone laughed at Dex's comment. Everyone but Chris. Slightly defeated, Chris probed, "What's so funny?"

"Your flameout, Cowboy!" chided Dex.

"The lady's a foreigner, and I don't think she likes tall, handsome

Texans," Chris replied defensively.

Carla, the articulate Columbia grad from the company's NYC office, retorted, "Chris, you wilted quicker than a snowflake in the Texan sun."

"Let's see you do better, Carla."

"Sorry Ryan, my hubby wouldn't approve, or on second thought, maybe he would. But I don't roll that way, not that there's anything wrong with rolling any way you choose."

Carla Pushkin had a special place in Ryan's heart. She had tremendous EQ, a valuable skill for a salesperson. Her customers loved her. He poached her from Oracle, where they worked together in a prior life. Her territory was New Jersey, New York, Pennsylvania, and Connecticut. Like Vanessa, she was over-educated for her role. Carla was married to Mark, a prominent New York City eye surgeon, and she spent most evenings pursuing a graduate degree in psychology. Money wasn't her primary motivator, and Ryan knew he'd lose her when she earned her MS.

During joint sales calls, Carla enrolled Ryan in Mrs. Pushkin's Finishing School. She rounded out Ryan's rough Jersey-Bro edges by teaching him obscure etiquette lessons like, "When a revolving door is moving, the woman goes first; when it's not rotating, the man goes first to start it moving," and "on escalators, the man goes first so as not to compromise the ladies' posterior."

Amidst the gaiety, Chris issued a challenge, "Alright, Ryan, if you're such a stud muffin, how about you show us how it's done, boss man."

Ryan raised his hands in mock surrender, " I haven't been on the prowl for eighteen years, and bar chatter wasn't my forte back then. What do I say to her? Something corny, like, haven't I seen you someplace before? Or come here often?" Despite his protests, the crew wouldn't let him off the hook. Peer pressure, he thought, was like WiFi - you don't see it, but when you're connected to a bad network, the signals are all too clear.

Drawing a deep breath, Harman approached her. For a brief second, he was lost in the depths of her captivating hazel eyes. Mustering up his courage, he teased her with the first thing that came to mind: "Buy me a drink."

She arched an eyebrow, "Isn't it the other way around? Aren't you supposed to buy me a drink?"

Ryan noticed a slight Eastern European accent, then grinned, and relying on the quick-thinking improvisation skills that had served him so well in business, he responded, "I wouldn't want to do that to you.

"Do what?" She asked with a curious smile.

"Well, If I buy you a drink, we'd chat and laugh; I'm funny and a likable guy; I'd buy you another drink, we'd laugh some more, and after a few more rounds, I'd ask you to join me in my room up at the Drake; you'll be a little drunk, you'd feel tipsy and obligated, I wouldn't want to put you in that position."

She playfully narrowed her eyes, "Alright, cowboy. I'll buy you a drink."

Now Ryan's smile turned devilish as he figured out what to say next, "No, forget it. I don't want your drink."

"Wait, what? What now?"

And he calmly explained, "You see, you'll buy me a drink, we'll laugh, have another drink, and pretty soon…"

He was cut off as she grabbed him by the tie and pulled him until they were nose to nose. "Your move, funny boy."

Before Ryan could say another word, a rush of familiarity washed over him. The petite and feisty Carla was by his side, planting a peck on his cheek. "Honey, we need to get home. We only have the babysitter till eleven." The statement, though a playful jest, served as a stark reminder. Ryan's thoughts immediately drifted to Phoebe, his ten-year-old daughter. The evening's escapade might have to wait for another lifetime.

As they walked away, Carla said to him, "You looked like you needed some help there."

He looked into Carla's warm brown eyes, took a moment, and said, "Thank you for bailing me out. I had no idea how I was going to exit that gracefully."

Carla smiled and replied, "I knew you weren't going home with her. That's not who you are."

Ryan wasn't so sure about that as he thought, "I didn't enter that little chit-chat thinking it would lead anywhere… but that was close to the first time I ever thought I might cheat on Amy. Who knows where it would have gone if Carla hadn't pulled my ass out of the fire."

The moment the aiCheckmate team left Pippin's, a beautiful raven-haired temptress, seated at the bar, removed her mobile phone from her purse, dialed an international number, and said, "Almost, but not yet. I'll try again later tonight."

CHAPTER II

A KNOCK AT THE DOOR.

It was fifteen minutes past midnight, the Chicago skyline sprawled outside Ryan's luxurious hotel suite's window, the glittering city lights reflected on Lake Michigan below while casting moving shadows onto the polished oak floor. Peering down at Lakeshore Drive and Lake Michigan, his room, on the thirtieth floor of the Drake, was adorned with contemporary art and rich velvets in deep blues and soft grays.

A complimentary bottle of vintage champagne, a gift from the hotel GM for holding a group meeting at the Drake, sat chilling in an ornate ice bucket next to a plush velvet chaise.

Ryan stood five foot nine, built like a linebacker, and athletic, a testament to his track days. Salt-and-mostly-pepper hair, confident yet laid-back, with a quick wit, and sardonic humor. He wasn't an adonis, but he was not unattractive, with dark, almost black-piercing eyes that seemingly read your thoughts like an fMRI and a vibe that exuded confident competence. Harman had the uncanny ability to read humans.

He stood replaying the day's events in his mind. The sales meeting was a success, the team was gelling. And then there was that woman at the bar. Absorbed in his thoughts, he was suddenly snapped back to reality by a gentle knock. He opened the door to the dilemma he encountered at Pippin's. Her silhouette, backlit by the corridor lights, rendered him momentarily speechless.

"May I?" she asked with a coy smile, nodding towards the luxurious suite.

"May I what?"

"Come in."

Ryan hesitated momentarily, then responded, "Before anything else, I should tell you – I'm married." There was no Carla to bail him out in this room.

"Is talking a violation of your marital vows?" The woman replied with a raised eyebrow and a knowing smile.

Harman's mind began to whirl. The allure of the situation, the tension, the beautiful woman before him felt surreal, like a scene straight out of a movie or some cheap novel. Yet, the small voice in his head kept repeating: You have responsibilities. Remember your daughter. Remember the commitment, and as he kept repeating the thought in his mind, he felt that he was losing himself in the eyes of this woman's piercing gaze.

For as long as he could remember, Harman felt alone, even in a crowd. Few people, with the exception of his daughter and a small cadre of intimate friends, had the ability to fill that void. His adrenaline surged from the day's meeting and the events at Pipin's earlier this evening; Ryan wouldn't be able to fall asleep for hours. This beguiling, attractive woman was offering a pleasant alternative to watching the talking-head outrage machines on cable news. Why not? Against his better judgment, he said, "Come on in; I'll give you an hour; if you're happy just talking, you can keep me company until I'm ready for bed... come on in."

Pushing past him into the room, she made herself at home and poured herself a glass of champagne before sitting on the bed, cross-legged. Transfixed on her long legs in those open-toe Jimmy Choo stilettos, Harman took a seat on the chaise.

Harman, "So, what's up? Why are you here? Why now?"

"I thought we had unfinished business," Ryan, surprised and intrigued, played along.

Every step she took sent ripples of anxiety through his chest. Each movement, every laugh, every glance she threw his way added another layer of tension to the tightrope he was walking. Yet, alongside the anxiety was a flutter igniting a sensation he hadn't experienced in a very long time.

"Do you mind telling me your name? I'm not used to entertaining nameless strangers." Ryan was both intrigued and cautious. He was not an ugly man, but women like this, they just didn't throw themselves at him… not ever, as in never. He had no idea why he was putting himself in this position. He just knew he was dangerously tempting fate and had no intentions of infidelity.

"I'm Deandra, but call me Dee," taking a sip of her champagne.

"Okay, and how did you find me?"

"My friend, Sarah, your waitress at Pippin's, told me your name. When you charmed and then ditched me back there, you mentioned The Drake. So armed with the knowledge you were staying here and then handing twenty dollars to the hotel's desk clerk, voila... I'm here."

"Wow, are you a detective or a spy or something?" As he said that, his phone, still on do-not-disturb from the meeting, vibrated. He took a quick glance, and it was another call from Amy that would go unanswered. As he looked up, Dee rewarded him with a seductive, toothy smile and a laugh, supplying no answer to his query.

That response, or lack of response, raised more questions than it answered, yet Ryan felt incomprehensibly compelled to let her stay. "Dee, what brings you here… why me?"

Across the room, Dee's cool hazel eyes held Ryan's gaze, and his heartbeat raced like Buddy Rich's snare drum.

"Ryan, you had me back at Pippin's. Obviously, you wanted what you saw; I've never experienced a man who got as far as you had and then watched as he simply turned his back and walked away. What happened there? Why'd you leave?" Deandra looked into his eyes. "You said you're married, but the way your eyes look at me says that shouldn't be an obstacle. Are you happily married?"

"Hey, if you want me to say you're a very desirable woman, I will grant you that. I like what I see; you're goddamn beautiful, and I'm sure you know that. So yes, I like what I see; I like lots of things; I would love a Ferrari. I can't afford a Ferrari, and I'm not going to steal one. There's right, there's wrong. Stealing a Ferrari and cheating on my wife, the mother of my child, are both on the wrong side of right."

"That's not what I asked, Ryan. Are you happy in your marriage?"

He let out a heavy sigh, feeling the weight of memories pressing against him. Sixteen years ago, during his senior year at the University of Maryland, Ryan had encountered Amy Dalton at a fraternity party. Her beauty was dazzling, and he was immediately entranced, so much so that he saw past any flaws she might have had. Born into a prominent, old-money family from Baltimore, Maryland, Amy carried an aura of prestige. They became an exclusive item for the remainder of Ryan's senior year. Just before graduation, carried away by youthful passion, Ryan had proposed, and she had said yes. But the past five years bore little resemblance to the marital bliss they had once dreamt of.

"It's complicated. But marriage isn't just about happiness. It's about commitment, and I've made one."

Dee swirled her finger around her glass, provocatively cocked her head, "Well, that's commendable. That doesn't mean we can't get to know each other better. Show me yours, and I'll show you mine... tell me who Ryan is, and I'll tell you about Dee."

"Me? I'm a Jersey boy who learned how to put on a suit and tie."

Dee sips her champagne with a playful tone, "So, Ryan Harman from New Jersey, how did you get here? I mean, doing whatever you're doing in a luxury suite in a luxury hotel? How does a Jersey boy go from Exit Ten to the thirtieth floor of The Drake?"

Ryan stopped and thought for a moment and asked himself, "Huh? Did I give her an exit or even a town name?" and responded, "Easy; I muddled my way through High School, struggled my way through college, graduated, and under the threat of having to return to 'The Garden State' I begged my way into the rewarding world of technology sales."

"Why Maryland?" she asked.

One of my best friends went there, and when I visited it, I fell in love with the area and the school. Any place was an upgrade from Jersey.

Dee sipped her champagne and, in a playful tone, said, "So, Ryan Harman, Jersey boy. Who would've thought I'd share a champagne evening with a Captain of Industry?"

Ryan, chuckling and brushing off the playful jibe, "Captain of Industry... that's generous... I'm more of a grade-school lunchroom monitor."

Dee, raising an eyebrow, "Lunchroom monitors don't run sales and marketing for a venture-backed, tech darling like aiCheckmate."

A cold shiver ran down Ryan's spine. How much did she know? The questions continued to pelt him. Was this just innocent flirtation or something more? Was this a test? As much as he wanted to flee the situation, a part of him was rooted to the spot, both intrigued and terrified by the mysterious beauty.

Ryan, taken aback, "You've done your homework."

aiCheckmate? Ryan thought. I never mentioned my company. There's something off about her. I should send her packing now. But his loneliness and curiosity prevailed... against his better judgment, he continued. "Okay... now you. Go!"

It's a simple story: born and raised in Ukraine—a private boarding school outside London. Then, a little university in Providence, RI, called Brown.

"Boarding schools, and an Ivy. You're definitely out of my league."

Dee, laughing, "And you? Impressive, from Jersey's diners to scion of the software industry on the global stage. Quite the journey. And yet, here we are. In Chicago. It seems we've both strayed far from our origins, if not geographically, then socially."

Ryan sipped his drink and nodded, "Life's unpredictable. One day, you're hanging with a bunch of clowns who think they're in the cast of the Sopranos. Next, you're negotiating multi-million dollar software deals around the world. But tell me, come on, no BS, Dee from Ukraine, what brings you to my door tonight?"

Dee sipped her champagne: "Sometimes, it's not about the destination but the journey. And this? This is just a pit stop on my journey."

Ryan felt her answer was evasive; he smirked and remarked, "Funny, my journeys had pit stops in diners and pizza joints. Yours seem a bit more upscale."

Dee, winking, "What can I say? I've acquired a taste for the finer things."

Ryan, looking around the lavish room, "Clearly. By the way, you seem to know a bit about me. But you really haven't told me much about you. Why are you in Chicago?"

Dee, leaning back, "Ah, the beauty of mystery. Isn't it exhilarating? I'm a marketing consultant, and I'm here to present to a client."

Intrigued by Dee's air of mystery, Ryan ventured to ask, "Tell me about your journey from Ukraine to this night."

She hesitated for a split second, then replied, "I'm from Ukraine. But I've traveled quite a bit throughout my life."

"And how did you end up studying in a UK boarding school and then at Brown?"

Dee momentarily looked distant and bit her lip as if reminiscing about a time long past. "Well, it's a bit of a story. My family in Ukraine wasn't wealthy, not by any means. But my grandfather was a renowned chess master back in the day. He won several international tournaments and even coached some of the best players in the world. One of his students, an English gentleman with ties to some prestigious schools, was particularly fond of my grandfather and was forever indebted to him for his teachings. He offered to sponsor my education in England as a token of his gratitude. That's how I ended up at that posh boarding school."

"And Brown?"

She chuckled, "That was a stroke of luck and a bit of determination. I worked hard, really hard, at my school in England. I became one of the top students and secured a scholarship at Brown. I was always fascinated with American education and culture, so I jumped at the chance."

Ryan raised an eyebrow, "That's quite the journey. From Ukraine to England to the U.S., It's impressive."

Dee smiled, her eyes twinkling with a hint of mischief, "Life has a way of surprising you. Just when you think you've figured it all out, it throws a curveball your way."

As they shared stories, Ryan's guard remained up. The weight of his responsibilities, both personal and professional, loomed over him. But this interaction with Dee was just the beginning of the twists that awaited.

She stepped closer, her voice barely above a whisper, "You say you're in a committed relationship, Ryan. We all have commitments. But when's the last time you felt alive?"

He could feel the warmth of her breath, and it stirred something profound within him, a mixture of guilt and longing. "It's not about that. It's about doing what's right, especially for my daughter, Phoebe. I can't imagine doing anything that might risk my relationship with her."

Deandra gently traced a finger along his jaw. "You think giving into your desires would do that?"

Ryan looked down, battling the storm of emotions churning inside. "I don't know what would happen. But the fear of losing my daughter's respect, of disappointing her... it's too much."

She smiled, a hint of sadness in her eyes. "I understand. Sometimes, the things we want most are the very things that scare us most."

They stood in silence for a moment, surrounded by the room's elegant soft acoustic music, Ari Hest's "Strangers Again" was playing in the background. The city lights twinkled, casting a glow that reflected the internal conflict before them.

Finally, Ryan spoke, "Dee, you're a beautiful woman. I'm pretty sure you know that. But I can't – I won't – jeopardize my relationship with my family."

She nodded, accepting his words. "I respect that. And maybe it's better this way." She took his champagne glass, walked to the ice bucket, and poured more, bending over. Ryan admired her long, shapely legs. He tried not to stare.

"One more question," Ryan asked, "Why me?"

"I don't know," she replied, "I guess there's something about Ryan," with a grin. "Here," she said, handing him his full champagne flute. "One more drink, a few more minutes, and I'll leave you to think about the best night of your life you'll never have."

The next thing Ryan knew, he woke in his room to his seven a.m. alarm, head foggy and slightly aching, in a rumpled bed, smelling of the musk of bodies that had spent the night doing more than just sharing a drink. His memory of the past night was completely blank after he took that last drink. Yet this morning, he was alone, except for a rumpled bed, her perfume on his pillow wafting in the air.

While putting on his sweats and running shoes to prepare for his morning run, he noticed a slight white powder residue at the bottom of his empty champagne glass. And then he looked over at the desk… his laptop was open. Did he leave it open?

CHAPTER III
UNEXPECTED ENCOUNTERS

Still feeling groggy, Harman descended the steps of the grand, venerable hotel and began his run along the lakeshore. The invigorating chill of the forty-eight-degree early October morning slapped him in the face. He felt his mind clearing.

Passing by the tall glass spires of the bustling city, he replayed the prior night's events in his mind. The first day of the meeting was a success. His team, with no exceptions, were hitting on all cylinders. That woman… she kept invading his mind… last night, kept coming back to him, in a stinging memory like he'd kicked a wasp nest and a horde of angry wasps were seeking retribution inside his head. And then there were the unanswered messages from Amy. He was going to have to deal with that sometime.

He thought back to that day six years ago on a warm August afternoon when he first heard about aiCheckmate. Ryan and his wife were sitting on a Delaware Beach while Phoebe, their four-year-old daughter, made sandcastles with her summer beach crew. His phone rang.

"Harman," Ryan answered.

"Hi Ryan, Glad this number still works. This is Sebastian Mitchell."

"Seb! Been a long time." From Ryan's days at Oracle, Sebastian "Seb" Mitchell had been his main contact at the National Security Agency. He might just be the smartest man Ryan had ever met.

Seb was always impressed with Ryan. He wasn't just a sales schlepper. Ryan always made sure he understood Seb's requirements. Unlike most transactional schlocky salespeople, he had considerable technical knowledge, he answered questions honestly, even when his honesty shone a defective light on his product. He was whip-smart, a big-picture businessman, and Seb sensed Ryan played the long game… he wasn't transactional.

"Look, Ryan, I left the NSA, and you are one of the first people I'm calling because I'm starting a company. It's an AI cyber security software company. I know when you sold your startup, Network Entropy, you made significant bank. I was wondering if you figured out what you want to do next. Are you out of the game or ready for a new play?" Seb could hear the sound of the surf, the gulls, and the laughter of children playing on the other end of the phone. "Is this a good time?"

"Sure, I was just sitting here with my family, trying to figure out my next move."

Amy shot an annoyed look at her husband, who was supposed to be dedicating this beach time to the family. As Seb got to the point, "Ryan, I want you to be part of this. I can handle the engineering, but I need someone to run the business end. I want that someone to be you."

"I'll be back in town in two weeks," Ryan replied, flattered by Seb's interest and looking to placate his wife's no-business during family time rule. "Let's set up a meeting then."

When Ryan returned from the beach, he and Mitchell met in a Starbucks, came to terms, and in addition to accepting the job, Ryan and Seb shook hands on Ryan's offer to invest two hundred and fifty thousand dollars in the company.

Back on the early morning streets of Chicago, a car screeched to a halt, the driver leaning heavily on the horn, bringing Ryan's mind back to earth from the clouds. He waved an embarrassed apology and headed into the hotel to prep for day two of the meeting.

In his room, he entered the shower and began thinking through this morning's agenda. Today was focused on preparing the sales team to sell the company's newest product, Checkmate.

Checkmate promised to be the game-changing software that

would rocket Harman to the billionaires club. The system harnessed a vast arsenal of system attack knowledge and used AI to devise attacks that could penetrate the most secure systems.

In the wrong hands, Checkmate had the potential to devastate governments, economies, and infrastructure. For this reason, the United States Director of National Intelligence (DNI) mandated that all deliveries of Checkmate required DNI approval and could only be sold and used by an approved list of NATO and other Allied intelligence agencies.

He shook his head and brought his mind back to the now. He had a meeting to run. Ryan turned off the water, took a towel from the towel warmer rack, and began to suit up for day two of the sales meeting.

The gilded walls of The Drake's conference room shimmered in the dim light, reflecting the soft buzz of conversation as Ryan's team took their seats around the large mahogany table. It was one of those rooms that always impressed Ryan with its blend of vintage luxury and modern amenities. Ryan could hear the familiar hum of a projector warming up as he approached the room.

However, when he stepped inside, the last person he expected to see was Dee, busily adjusting a projector aimed at the wide screen against one wall. Ryan struggled to remain composed as Dee looked up briefly, a mischievous smile before she recovered and masked her expression with professional coolness.

"Oh, hello again," she said, looking completely rested, offering a smile that was slightly tight around the edges. "I hope you're having a good morning."

Ryan cleared his throat, attempting to dispel any potential suspicions from his team regarding his connection with Dee beyond their encounter at the bar the previous night. He addressed her, saying, "Dee, isn't it? I must admit, your presence here caught me by surprise."

She chuckled, "I get that a lot. My role can be quite... diverse. I'm here for a marketing presentation. Your team is here to develop marketing strategies for your new product, right?"

Ryan nodded, trying to cover his surprise. "Yes, the Checkmate product release. But I wasn't aware we had an external consultant on board."

"Your CEO, Seb, hired us to roll out this marketing plan to the sales team. Sometimes, it's good to get an outsider's perspective," Dee said as she made the final adjustments to the projector. The first slide displayed a sleek logo with the words 'Korolev Strategies', her apparent firm.

As Ryan's team began to settle in, there were murmurs of recognition. "Damn, Korolev Strategies. These are the people who transformed companies like Atlassian, Salesforce, and ChatGPT, among others," Sarah, the team's sales operations manager, whispered to Ryan. "They were the team behind AlphaDog's transformation from a cute little puppy to a global unicorn in two years. They transformed a host of other companies in the last ten years or so."

Dee cleared her throat, drawing the room's attention. "Good morning, everyone. I'm Deandra Volkova, but you can call me Dee. I represent Korolev Strategies. Today, I'm here to offer insights into how your Checkmate product fits into the cyber-security landscape and how to position it to win."

As Dee explained a complex marketing strategy, Chris Long, still smarting from being turned down the night before at the bar, interrupted, "You know, Ms. Korolev, as a marketing consultant, I'd like your feedback. Would you help me understand why my marketing proposal to you last night failed? How could I have done better to let you understand you should take advantage of my southern hospitality? What should I have done to get you to say yes?"

There was an awkward pause and a hush in the room as tension grew. A few team members exchanged uncomfortable glances while others tried to stifle their chuckles. Carla playfully threw a Sharpie at Chris.

Dee's eyes flashed, but she maintained her composure. "Mr. Long," she began, her tone dripping with icy politeness, "I appreciate your attempt at humor. However, my aim today is to help your company launch your new product, not to discuss personal flaws and failures."

Chris raised an eyebrow, visibly taken aback by her response. Before he could retort, Ryan stepped in. "Chris, let's keep this professional. Dee's insights are valuable, and we're here to work."

Chris, a former all-conference college football player, leaned back, clearly not used to being put in his place. "Just making conversation," he drawled.

The presentation resumed, but the dynamic in the room had shifted. Evidently, Dee was not someone to be taken lightly, and she commanded professional and personal respect.

The presentation flowed smoothly, with Dee deftly handling questions and interjections. Ryan was impressed by her depth of knowledge, charisma, and how she commanded the room.

During a brief coffee break, he approached her with a determined look. "Dee, I had no idea you were hired to work with us."

She raised an eyebrow, half-smiling. "There's a lot you don't know about me, Ryan. But maybe, in time, you will."

As the day wore on, Ryan found himself even more intrigued by the enigma that was Dee. She was no longer just the beautiful stranger he had met the previous night. His spidey senses screamed danger; this was a black widow spider of a woman, a force to be reckoned with, and Ryan realized he had just embarked on a journey that would challenge everything he thought he knew.

CHAPTER IV
HOME TURMOIL

After a tiring day, Ryan boarded a late afternoon United Airlines flight from O'Hare, headed to Washington Reagan National Airport. The dim cabin lights cast a mellow glow, and the low hum of the plane's engines was almost hypnotic. It gave him time to reflect on the whirlwind of events he had experienced. As the plane touched down and he collected his carry-on, the weight of reality began to sink in. He had difficult issues, crap he'd been avoiding, waiting for him at home, and no amount of delay at the airport would change that.

Upon exiting the airport, he hopped into his Uber for the thirty-minute ride to his home. The George Washington Parkway traffic was relatively light as he passed the exit for CIA headquarters. Five minutes later, the car turned onto Cabin John Bridge, leaving Virginia and crossing into Maryland on the Washington Beltway. The car approached the upscale suburb of Potomac, Maryland, with its meticulously landscaped gardens. The grand homes, occupied by senators, congresspersons, lobbyists, lawyers, and prominent doctors, stood as silent witnesses to the many stories unfolding behind their closed doors. Ryan's home was no different, with its sprawling lawn, elegant facade, and circular driveway.

Ryan turned the key in the front door and pushed it open, stepping into the familiar warmth of his home. Almost immediately, he felt a rush of movement as a small figure darted toward him, jumping up into his arms and wrapping her arms around his neck. Looking into her smiling face, he was met with the bright blue eyes of his daughter, Phoebe, her blond hair a disheveled mess of golden curls.

"Daddy!" she exclaimed, her voice filled with relief. "I missed you so much!"

"I missed you too, sweetie. How's my little angel been?"

Phoebe's joy dimmed slightly. "Mommy was out shopping half the time, and when she was home, she was on her phone or computer. She spent no time with me. It was pretty much just me and Rita," Phoebe's Ugandan nanny, "on our own. Can we ride our bikes to the Village to get ice cream?"

"It's a little late tonight. We can do that tomorrow; we'll ride in and get pizza and ice cream for lunch. Okay?"

Ryan's wife, Amy, was a stay-at-home mom with an overbooked, active social schedule. That left Phoebe's daily care, cleaning, and other sundry chores to Rita. Fortunately, Rita was a fabulous companion, and Phoebe adored her, but Rita didn't ride a bike.

Ryan sighed internally. It wasn't Phoebe's first complaint about her mother's inattentiveness. Amy rarely had time for Ryan or their daughter. He squeezed Phoebe tighter, whispering comforting words into her ear, "I love you, bug, and so does Mommy."

As he set Phoebe down and began to remove his coat, he felt a chilling presence behind him. Turning, he found his wife, Amy, standing with her arms crossed, a look of fury etched on her face.

"Where were you last night, Ryan?" she snapped. "I tried calling you over a dozen times. No answer, no texts, nothing."

Ryan looked to Phoebe, who was cowering as she anticipated another round of tense discussions between her mom and dad.

Ryan hesitated. He had indeed missed several calls from Amy the previous night. Still, he had been so engrossed in his evening with Dee and then the unexpected turn of events at the conference today that he had "unintentionally" left his phone on silent. Although to himself, he admitted he deliberately avoided the call and the inevitable fight that would ensue. Why fight with her last night and again when he got home when he could have both fights today? The choice was clear. Go for the one-for; opting for one fight instead of two.

"I'm sorry, Amy," he began, choosing his words carefully. "I had a late-night work meeting, and my phone was on silent. It slipped my mind to check."

Amy's eyes narrowed. "A meeting? At night? Since when does your work keep you out till the early hours without a single call or message?"

Ryan could feel the weight of Amy's skepticism. "It was unplanned. We had a consultant from out of town, and things ran later than expected."

"Was she pretty?" Amy shot back, her voice dripping with venom.

There she goes again, he thought, insinuating infidelity. Even with his steadfast commitment, her doubts always lingered. It's almost not worth it being faithful. She'd accused him of cheating many times before, but because of last night, Ryan was caught off guard. "Wha— Amy, I never said it was a she. What are you talking about?" He wondered if he could still claim an unblemished streak of fidelity.

"You heard me," Amy hissed. "You think I don't know what goes on at these so-called 'business meetings'?"

Phoebe, sensing the tension between her parents, tugged at Ryan's sleeve. "Daddy, can we go play in my room?"

Ryan crouched down, looking into Phoebe's worried eyes. "Of course, sweetheart. Let's give Mommy some space."

As Ryan and Phoebe ascended the stairs, Amy's voice rang out. "We're not done, Ryan. You've been distant for months, and last night was the last straw. We need to talk." Ryan thought, here's another one of Amy's numerous last straws, me distant? All Amy needs me for is to entertain and drive a carpool for our daughter.

He paused, glancing back. He could see the hurt and anger in Amy's eyes. Their marriage had been strained for a while, with both of them leading busy lives and rarely finding time for each other. Last night's absence was just the latest in a series of grievances.

"Amy," Ryan started, his voice firm but quiet, "we'll talk. Just not in front of Phoebe."

The silence that followed was thick with unsaid words and emotions. The happiness of returning home to Phoebe was overshadowed by the clear understanding that Ryan's marriage was hanging by a thread. He had come to the realization that they hadn't fallen out of love. That the connection between them as a couple might have been based more on physical attraction than genuine love. He understood lust had a half-life without love as a foundation.

As Ryan came to bed, Amy was asleep and as far on the right side of the bed as she could be without falling to the floor. The message was clear. Don't touch me, don't bother me, stay away from me. For the last year or so, this had been his life in his bedroom.

CHAPTER V

REUNION CROSS THE POND

Two days later, Ryan boarded a British Airways flight from Dulles International to Heathrow London. He settled into his business class seat with the time and space to think about his career, deteriorating relationship with Amy, the implications of a possible divorce, and what that would mean to Phoebe, and then there was Dee. Dee... she kept invading his thoughts as he played that Chicago night over and over again in his head like a TikTok video stuck in a loop. He knew he should run away from her like he was anchoring the state finals of his sixteen-hundred-meter relay, but Dee had become an earworm that nested deep in his brain.

He filed the worm in a compartment of his brain. He would deal with it later and began planning the upcoming Europe, Middle East, and Africa (EMEA) sales meeting in London. It had been months since he'd seen his old friend, Raj Patel, aiCheckmate's Vice President of Global Sales. Raj reported to Ryan and managed the EMEA and Asia Pac teams.

Eleven years ago, Harman was in London to hire a salesperson for his startup Network Entropy. Patel heard Ryan was hiring, tracked Ryan down, and convinced him he needed a Vice President instead of a salesperson and that Raj was the VP he required. Raj could sell million-dollar sound systems to the deaf, thousand-foot sailing yachts to desert Bedouins, and a Vice President of Global Sales to a man looking for a salesperson.

Raj's parents immigrated to Scotland from Mumbai. An honor graduate from the University of Glasgow, Raj was born and raised in Edinburgh, where his parents ran a successful Indian Bistro. He was intelligent, hardworking, dependable, loyal, and anything but a yes man, all the qualities Harman valued and common traits to his small cadre of trusted friends and confidants. Patel had a thick Scottish brogue, could drink any man or woman and possibly many elephants under any table, and just might be the most entertaining and funny human being on Earth.

As he disembarked, the gray clouds hanging over Heathrow Airport did little to dampen Ryan's spirit. He'd come to appreciate these work trips as an escape from the tumultuous atmosphere of his home.

A familiar face emerged from the crowd as Ryan navigated the bustling terminals, searching for the exit. Raj Patel was waiting for him, wearing a finely tailored suit and a mischievous grin. The two men closed the distance quickly, sharing a warm hug that spoke of years of camaraderie.

"Och aye, look at you, all tanned and dapper!" Raj exclaimed, patting Ryan on the back.

Ryan chuckled and joked, "That's weird. It's nine in the morning, and I don't smell the whisky on you yet. Are you off the sauce?."

Raj smirked, "Aye, don't let the smell fool ya, mate. I have me a bottle of the Talisker waiting in the car." Patel winked and dropped the levity, "It's a long ride to the hotel, and London traffic this time of day is a nightmare."

The duo made their way to the parking lot, where a sleek black Jaguar awaited them. As Raj navigated the car through traffic, the two old friends fell into easy conversation, reminiscing about past sales conferences, shared successes, and the occasional hilarious mishap.

Ryan, looking to stir the pot a bit, teased, "Remember the time in Hong Kong when you tried to impress that client with your Mandarin and ended up ordering a hundred duck tongues instead of duck rice?"

Raj burst out laughing, "Oh, don't remind me! But in my defense, the client found it hilarious. Closed the deal right there!"

"And who ended up paying for those hundred duck tongues?"

Ryan prodded, his eyes twinkling with mischief.

With a big grin, Raj replied, "Aye, it's been too long, Ryan. I haven't seen you since our sales meeting in Amsterdam last April. Life's been treatin' me well, cannae complain. And you? How's things Stateside?"

"Busy as ever, but I've missed our global escapades. Some day, I'm going to write a book, 'Travels with Raj.' But to answer your question, business is great, Phoebe is great, and Amy is still Amy.

Raj was serious for a moment and said, "I know how much that pains you, Ryan, and I'm sorry for that." Then, to make things more upbeat, he changed the subject, "Remember our last sales conference in Amsterdam, the escapade where you couldn't tell the difference between a bicycle and a boat? The entire team laughed like banshees as you tried to cycle through the canals thanks to a wee bit too much liquid Dutch Courage."

Ryan laughed: "Hey, in my defense, I thought the bike was a paddle boat."

"Hoots, laddie! Ye were truly blootered that night, ye mistook a mop for a bellman at Hotel Krasnapolsky!"

"Yeh, that night, I was, or I guess I should say, I thought I was invincible, and I believed I could fly. I was no worse than you, my friend, when you thought you could pull off wearing that silly dress to your wedding.

Raj's eyes lit up with mischief: "Ah, the Highland Wedding to Nina, the love of my life! A grand day that was."

Ryan, smirked: "Indeed! Who could forget the sight of you with that entrance, landing in a helicopter at the wedding site and exiting in that silly checkered mini-skirt you call a kilt."

Raj, feigned indignation: "Oi! That's a traditional Highland dress, ye cheeky bugger! But I'll give it to ya, not everyone can pull off the look, especially with these legs." He gestures comically to his legs.

Ryan laughed, "And the food! Haggis Masala?"

Raj, groaned, "We did not have the Haggis lad. Listen, man, my mum's secret recipe, Scotch Pie Masala, is renowned throughout these isles, and I will not have you denigrate her cooking!"

Ryan replied, "It's a joke, buddy; the food was absolutely the high point of the wedding, your skirt notwithstanding. Half Scottish brogue, half Indian charm. That's our Raj."

The two friends continued their banter, filling the car with laughter as they made their way to the Marriott Regent's Park. It would be clear to anyone who watched that these two shared a solid professional relationship and a deep personal bond.

The car rolled to a stop in front of the hotel, and Raj turned to Ryan, sincerity in his eyes. "It's great to have you here, Ryan. We've missed you on this side of the pond."

Ryan placed a hand on Raj's shoulder, grateful for the genuine connection. "It's good to be back, Raj. Thanks for the ride. Let's make sure this sales meeting drives results. Can you join me in the bar this evening? I want to review your team's performance before we start tomorrow."

And with that, Ryan grabbed his bags and walked into the hotel as Raj called through the window, "I'll be back at eight."

CHAPTER VI

STRATEGIES AND SUSPICIONS

He unpacked, laid down on the bed for a quick nap, and reminisced about how he got there.

He was born and raised in a middle-class family in central New Jersey. Like the Mason-Dixon line, New Jersey was divided by the Pork Roll/Taylor Ham line. Pork Roll in the New York City-influenced north, and Taylor Ham in the Philadelphia-influenced south. Harman grew up just north of that line, a mere forty-five-minute drive from Manhattan.

He was a distracted student at JP Stevens High School in Edison, New Jersey, just getting by with barely passing grades. His frustrated middle-class parents and teachers recognized his intelligence and found it sorely wasted by his lackadaisical attention to detail, homework, and studying. Every report card featured the wasted potential comment.

In the middle of his junior year, he realized that college was his path out of New Jersey, which meant he had to become a student. Motivation was the key, he upped his GPA enough that by his senior year, he was accepted to the freshman class of The University of Maryland.

He did just enough work at Maryland to earn a degree... barely. When he graduated, he discovered that a college degree was not a free pass to a rewarding career in business. For weeks after graduation, he struggled to find a job, realizing too late that his grades were an obstacle to any job better than Starbucks Barista... a career unacceptable to his high-society fiancée and both sets of the couple's parents.

Ryan's parents gave him an ultimatum. He had two weeks to find a job worthy of his parents' four-year college investment in his education, or he would have to move back home to New Jersey. Harman was never going back to New Jersey. He had often joked that Baja New York, his term for his home state, was the best state to be from and not in.

That week, with newfound motivation, or maybe desperation, he walked into the Oracle Software office in Reston, Virginia, without an appointment and told the receptionist he would not leave until he met with a sales manager. He sat in the lobby for a little over an hour. When he finally entered, Chuck Rothman stepped forward, shook Ryan's hand, explained he was one of the company's sales managers, and brought Ryan back to his office.

Rothman inquired about Ryan's sales experience. Ryan replied, "Well, there was the time I bought three hundred, about-to-be-out-of-style, expensive-looking shirts from a cut-rate wholesaler in New York City and then sold them out of my trunk at a McDonald's parking lot for thirty dollars each." He explained when potential buyers asked him, "'Where did you get these?'" He had a standard reply, "Hey, look, I don't ask where you get your clothes. Don't ask me where I get mine," implying they fell off the back of a proverbial truck.

"Besides that, Mr. Rothman, I have no sales experience."

Relevant sales experience, maybe not, Chuck thought to himself, but there was one thing this brash kid did have: chutzpah. Is that enough to justify hiring this kid? "Unlike many companies, we don't have a sales training program, so we hire experienced people from industry. I'm just not sure I can take a chance on you, Ryan."

Fearing he'd have to move back home, with his back up against the deadline, Harman pitched his heart out. "Look, you probably have salespeople doing all kinds of things that don't generate revenue. I'll do that for them. I'll carry your salespeople's bags until you think I'm ready to sell on my own. I'll work for nothing until you think I have the ability to earn my keep."

Rothman took the chance, hired the brash kid, and all of a sudden, the world changed for Ryan. He found himself thoroughly engaged with the work. He realized if he understood the inner workings of computers and software, he could use that knowledge to motivate customers to buy product, which generated commissions. He finally understood he wasn't dumb or lazy. He attributed his poor school performance to the disconnect between learning theory to any practical application in the real world. He also found out he was a computer savant.

So when Rothman assigned him a worthless patch… aka territory, Harman turned worthless into two million dollars of revenue in his first year, and in his third year, he was managing a sales team of ten men and women, all at least decade his seniors.

One more stop on the way to aiCheckmate, he and one of the engineers from Oracle co-founded a startup, Network Entropy. They raised twelve million dollars from top Silicon Valley venture firms, New Enterprise Associates and Menlo Ventures, and six years later, they sold the company to a larger competitor for a quarter of a billion dollars.

The buzzing of his phone alarm roused Ryan from his nap. He looked at the time, cleaned up, and left to meet Raj at the bar.

The Regency Park Marriott's bar emanated a soft glow with its warm, wooden undertones and plush seating. Ryan and Raj found a quiet corner, away from the murmur of patrons, offering them the space to deep-dive into the meeting's intricacies. The bartender served them their drinks—a Talisker scotch for Raj and a Woodford Manhattan for Ryan.

"To old times and to a successful sales meeting," Raj toasted, raising his glass.

Ryan clinked his glass with Raj's, "To dominating the EMEA market."

"No, Ryan, To dominating the world!"

With pleasantries exchanged, Raj spread a folder on the table with charts, graphs, and performance data about the sales reps.

"Let's start with the good news," Raj began, pointing at a bar chart. "Emma Fitzgerald is set to crush her numbers. Honestly, she has her clients eating out of her hands. I wish we could clone her."

Ryan nodded, recalling Emma's resume, "Her background from Manchester and her degree in international business seems to serve her well here in London."

"Absolutely," Raj agreed. "She has that charm, with smarts, a genuine interest in the clients, and it shows in her performance."

Lukas Müller's performance chart was next. "Lukas is consistent. His detailed approach, tailored solutions, and fluency in German, Dutch, and English make him an asset in his patch."

Ryan leaned in, "Is he set to meet his numbers?"

Raj sighed, "He's on track. Lukas is very diligent, and the clients trust him. He's never going to be our top rep, but he's consistent, solid, and trustworthy."

Ryan replied, "Every sales team needs a no-drama, steady performers like Lukas." Ryan's finger landed on Prague. "Martina Novakova. She's still a bit green?"

"She's new, but there's promise," Raj said. "She's adapting quickly and understands the tech industry and where we add value. The Eastern European market seems to respond well to her. She has the makings of a rock star. My only worry is that she works all hours day and night… Aye, if we can keep her from burning out, she'll give Emma a run for her money next year."

"I have confidence in you, Raj, to coach her through that."

Raj moved swiftly to the next name, not wanting to belabor the point, "Now, Avi Cohen—nothing to worry about. He's making his numbers again. Tel Aviv's market is practically in his pocket."

Avi, Ryan's oldest friend, was a Sabra, born in Tel Aviv, Israel; he moved to the United States after his parents died in a terrorist bus bombing and lived with an aunt from the time he was thirteen until graduating from the University of Maryland. Ryan and Avi had a history. They ran track together in High School. After graduating from college, Avi returned to Israel to join the Israeli Defense Forces, where he served as an Intelligence Officer. Avi left the service while wounded in the Lebanese July War.

Ryan gave Raj a serious look, "Raj, I know I suggested you hire Avi. I want to ensure you understand that Avi's a friend, but he's your rep. You manage and hold him accountable like any other salesperson. Avi knows that while I love him, he can't use me as a shield.."

"Nae issues, Ryan. Avi's got me respect 'cause he's earned it, not because I reckon it's what you want to hear."

They both paused when Raj's finger pointed to Stockholm; he hesitated over Elin Svenson's name. Raj's expression turned grave. "The Baltic... Elin... I'm concerned, Ryan. She's not hitting her numbers. Her account reports have more holes in them than Swiss Cheese. Sometimes, I think she's more Swiss than Swede. Her forecasts are less accurate than most horoscopes."

Ryan frowned, "You think she's bullshitting you?"

"I reckon," Raj lowered his voice, "that she might be a better fiction novelist than a sales lass. Her first book might hae three big accounts." He slid a paper toward Ryan with three company names listed:

- GalleriaTech Innovations
- Takin Digital Solutions
- The Swedish Defense Ministry

"She says she's got the BANT nailed."

aiCheckmate used a process known as BANT to qualify progress in accounts. BANT is an acronym where the "B" stands for Budget. Is there sufficient budget to fund a sale? "A" stands for Authority. How are decisions made, and who makes the decisions? Do we know who is friend or foe? "N" stands for Need. Has the need been identified, and does the product address the prospect's pains? And "T" stands for Timing. What is the timeline for making a decision and implementing a solution?

"Tomorrow, durin' her account review, we need tae press her, delve deep intae her detailed plans, and check her claims."

Ryan exhaled, troubled. "I had such high hopes for her. After her account review tomorrow, if we still don't buy what she's selling… she's out."

Raj looked grim, "There's more. Now that we finally made Andre Dupont available to industry, I'm wantin' tae bring in a replacement."

With a skeptical look, Ryan said, "I'm not sure we need to replace him. Lukas is covering that territory now, and he seems to be handling it just fine. If we do, hire someone, we're not hiring in France again; those employee protection regulations are too brutal. We need to be able to hire and fire fast. I've learned my lesson—no more employees based in France.

As Raj prepared to reply, his eyes opened wide. Ryan smelled something familiar as he felt a hand on his back. Dee bent down to Ryan's eye level; he felt her hot breath as she said, "Can I buy you a drink,' harking back to that night at Pipin's.

Ryan felt a mix of exhilaration and apprehension, his gaze piercing sharply into hers.

Dee said, "Come on, Ryan, I'm teasing you. I'm here to present to your sales team at your meeting here. Seb hired us to do all three regions. I'm on the agenda the day after tomorrow, but I figured I'd get here early and ease into the time change."

"Fantastic," Ryans, attempting to distance himself from temptation, replied in a tone that straddled sarcasm and anticipation. "Raj, meet Dee, she presented to our US team in Chicago last week, and she's here to meet with your team.

Raj, looked her up and down like he was evaluating a prized Angus Heifer, "Naece to meet ye, young lass. I'm lookin' forward tae spendin' time wi' ye. Good quality time."

"Now, if you'll excuse us, we're doing business here," interjected Ryan.

Dee excused herself from the two men and made her way to the bar. Her conservatively tailored blue business suit highlighted her figure, confidence, and grace. As she walked away, Ryan took notice of the heads that turned and watched her take a seat.

Ryan turned back to Raj, who was exhibiting his trademarked version of a shit-eating grin. "Hmmm, things are takin' a turn for the worse wi' Amy, a reckon ah've just unearthed the cause."

"No, Raj, you know what's been going on with Amy and me has been going on for years. Hell, she skipped your wedding. This lady has nothing to do with my Amy troubles." Ryan had no secrets from his trusted confidants and shared the details… all the details of the evening at the Drake with Raj.

Raj whistled softly and said, "I smell trouble, mister; you're playing with matches in a tub full of gasoline."

"I'm going to bed, Raj. Alone, I might add. I didn't sleep much on the plane, and I'm getting up early for a run in the morning before our meeting."

CHAPTER VII

MORNING RUN REVELATIONS

The early morning sun was still low on the horizon, casting a gentle golden hue over London. Slipping on his running shoes, he felt the familiar comfort and flexibility they offered, preparing him for the miles ahead.

Upon reaching the hotel lobby, he stopped short. Dee, her dark hair pulled back into a tight ponytail. He noticed that even with no makeup, she was a knock-out. Dee was lacing up her bright pink running shoes. He couldn't help but notice how her athletic attire complemented her toned physique.

"Morning," she greeted without looking up. Once her eyes met his, she flashed a playful smile. "Looks like we had the same idea. Fancy a running partner?"

Ryan hesitated momentarily, considering his options before deciding there was no downside, he finally nodded, "Sure, why not?"

They took off toward Regent's Park, breathing in the aromas of nearby cafes, the rhythmic pounding of their feet on the pavement acting as a backdrop to their conversation. The park was still relatively quiet at this hour, with only a few other early birds scattered about.

As they entered the park, Ryan breathed in the smell of fresh-cut, dew-covered grass, "Didn't take you for a morning person," Ryan remarked, attempting to make light conversation over the soft din of the park's sprinkler system.

Dee laughed, "I'm not, usually. But with the time difference, it seemed like a good idea to get moving."

They continued at a steady pace. As they neared the famous rose gardens, Dee slowed down a little, allowing for deeper conversation. "You seemed pretty tense at the bar last night."

Passing two fellow early morning joggers, thinking about the improbable coincidences of the numerous unexpected encounters with this woman, he sighed, "It's just... complicated. Between the sales meeting, team dynamics, and then you showing up..."

"Didn't think I'd ruffle any feathers just by walking into a room," Dee joked. But seeing his serious expression, she continued, "Look, about Pipin's... It was unexpected for both of us."

Ryan took a deep breath, releasing it slowly. "It wasn't just about Pipin's, Dee. It's everything else going on. And then seeing you the next day, it was... a lot to process."

"I get it," Dee replied, a hint of vulnerability in her eyes. "For what it's worth, I didn't know you were going to be at that bar that night. I wasn't expecting you or your team to be there. And if I did, I wouldn't have just thrown myself into the mix."

"What's your game, Dee?"

"No game, Ryan, I just am."

They jogged in silence for a few minutes, letting the cool morning air envelop them. The serenity of Regent's Park, with its chirping birds and gentle breeze, seemed to ease the tension between them.

Dee finally broke the silence, "Listen, we're both professionals. Let's keep it that way during the meetings. And after... we can figure things out."

Ryan nodded, "Dee, let me make this clear: our relationship is business; there is no after. There is no Us to figure out."

By the time they circled back to the hotel, the sun was fully up, casting a brighter light over the day. There was a new understanding between Ryan and Dee, a subtle truce, at least for the time being.

As they approached the hotel's entrance, Dee turned to Ryan, a hint of mischief in her eyes. "Race you to the door?"

Ryan chuckled, "You're on!" And with that, they both sprinted, the complexities of the previous week momentarily forgotten. The duo reached the hotel's entrance, panting slightly from their impromptu race. Ryan, ex-track star, was about to declare a tie when a familiar voice pierced the air.

"Well, isn't this a surprise?" The tone was icy, betraying no emotion. Elin Svenson stood just a few steps away, dressed impeccably in a sharp business suit, her blonde hair pulled back into a tight bun. A portfolio clutched to her chest was a shield of sorts, and her gaze was locked onto Dee with an intensity that was hard to read.

Ryan cleared his throat, feeling the weight of the situation. "Elin," he began, "This is Dee. She's presenting our Checkmate marketing plan at the sales meeting tomorrow."

Elin's gaze lingered on Dee for an extra second before she extended her hand with practiced politeness, "Pleasure." She looked between Ryan and Dee, eyeing them suspiciously, and added, "How's Amy?" Elin had developed a relationship with Amy in company meetings that included spouses and spouse equivalents, partners, or whatever the proper term was these days.

Ryan thought about Elin's disingenuous sweetness and thought, I wonder if the Swedish immigrants brought Minnesota-nice to the midwest?

Not to be outdone with dripping sincerity, Dee interrupted and smiled brightly. "I've heard good things about the work and progress the EMEA team was making. Your CEO, Mr. Mitchell, hired my firm to work on the marketing rollout for the Checkmate initiative. My job is to help you build on your success."

A flicker of annoyance crossed Elin's eyes, but her voice remained steady. "Do we need help? That's an interesting accent. Are you Russian?"

"No, Elin, born and raised in Ukraine. It's Ukrainian."

As a native of the Baltic, Elin knew her regional accents; she thought to herself, "Sounds more Russian to me."

Sensing the mounting tension, Ryan interjected. "I need to head up and get ready for the meeting. Elin, see you at the meeting later; I look forward to your account review. Dee, we'll see you tomorrow."

He quickly moved toward the elevators, stopped, turned, and said, "Dee, we're having dinner at Goodman Canary Wharf tonight. Dinner starts at 19:30 British time. Why don't you join us and meet the team before you present tomorrow?"

"I'd be delighted."

The elevator arrived, he entered, and as the doors closed, he couldn't help but wonder about the chain of events he had unknowingly set into motion.

CHAPTER VIII

SALES MEETING SHOWDOWN

The Regent's Park Marriott's mundane conference room filled with the hum of anticipation as the sales team settled into their seats. The room was dissected by sliding cloth walls in order to transform the large "Grand Ballroom" into a smaller, more intimate space. The morning sunlight streamed through the windows, casting a bright glow on the long, gleaming conference table.

Harman stood in the front of the room, the team's eyes all on him; he, in turn, looked at each, individually, one at a time, holding their gazes. He removed his suit jacket, rolled up his sleeves, and said, "I'm proud of the work and results this team has produced so far this year. The company appreciates your efforts. We're here today to track progress, understand, refine, and develop your account strategies. Understand what tools we can offer to help you win business. We are not just here to learn about your current target accounts. Think of this as an exercise to hone your skills and develop best practices for the future. Don't be afraid to be vulnerable; admit what you don't know… otherwise, we impede the learning process. We're all here to learn. Even Raj and me."

"Raj and I value effort, curiosity, assumptions based on facts, and an openness to questioning assumptions. In these reviews, making inaccurate assumptions based on partial data is okay. Making assumptions based on no data or, worse, fabricated data is unacceptable. So, let's hear your plans to crush your numbers and work together here to ensure exceptional results. Raj?"

With that, Harman sat, and Raj, dressed in a conservative blue pinstripe banker suit accented with a Royal Stewart Tartan tie, took his place at the front of the conference room's long, black walnut burl boardroom table. "Aye, team, ye heard whit Laird Harman said;

now, let's get goin'. First up, Emma Fitzgerald."

Emma's presentation was succinct and exuded confidence. She walked them through her client interactions, showcased impressive numbers, provided insights into her strategy, and deftly handled questions from Raj and Ryan. The room erupted in applause as she concluded.

Raj nodded and said, "Well done, lassie. Mak' sure tae tell Ryan or maself who or what ye need tae seal the McKesson deal. That's a grand one. Alright now, yer turn, Lukas."

Lukas Müller followed. His detailed, Teutonic, analytical approach mirrored his meticulous nature. He elaborated on his strategies and how he navigated the German and Benelux markets, securing trust and business. The room acknowledged his efforts with appreciative nods and returned the team's appreciation with a curt bow.

Martina Novakova, though relatively new, brought fresh perspectives and vitality to the floor. Her understanding of the tech industry and the Eastern European market was evident. Ryan admired that she was quick to admit when she didn't know something. The feedback she received was positive, with a few constructive critiques.

Ryan looked at Martina, then at Raj, and nodded, signaling to Raj that this lady had the right stuff.

Avi Cohen's presentation mirrored his reputation as an accomplished sales professional. His deep understanding of Israeli defense and intelligence agencies and mastery of aiCheckmate's product market fit was evident as he laid out his achievements and projections. His performance garnered unanimous approval.

Intentionally, Raj and Ryan had agreed that they'd save Elin for last. Raj motioned to Elin, "You are up, Elin."

Elin Svenson took a moment to compose herself before she began. She started confidently, laying out her progress with territory and account plans. Her slides showcased the apparent growth and interactions she had with GalleriaTech Innovations, Takin Digital Solutions, The Swedish Defense Ministry, and three other smaller accounts.

However, as Elin's presentation progressed, Ryan and Raj exchanged skeptical glances.

She claimed to have identified, spoken with and ascertained the process and disposition of the five individuals in the Swedish Defense Ministry's decision-making hierarchy. Her confidence broke down under questioning by Raj. Her story didn't hold together. There was hushed embarrassment in the room from the other reps as they all avoided eye contact.

Ryan decided to probe deeper. "Elin, can you provide more details about your interaction with Dolf, the Cyber Security Chief? Specifically, what is his criteria for making a decision?"

Elin hesitated, her confidence wavering slightly. "Um, well, the main decision criteria is cost, and he seemed favorably disposed to our proposal."

Raj said, "I've been askin' ye tae get me in a meetin' wi' him, and Hans Ericskonn, the ultimate decision maker for the past three weeks. We never had that meetin'. So, when did ye hae this process chat?"

Elin's voice quivered, "It was in... we... um, did it over email."

Raj replied, "Why wasnae I copied on these emails? Ye've got yer laptop; please pull up the emails."

Ryan, intending to avoid the corrosive effect of disrespecting an errant team member in front of the group, interrupted. "Elin, let's take this offline after the meeting."

One of Ryan's cardinal rules was to praise in public and criticize in private.

Raj stood and said, "Thank ye, laddies and lassies; wi' the account reviews all wrapped up, we'll be takin' a wee twenty-minute coffee brekkie before we dive intae discussin' the competitive landscape."

Ryan leaned over and whispered to Raj, who nodded subtly. It was clear they'd heard enough. While the team was in the midst of a short coffee break, Ryan motioned for Raj and Elin to follow him into a smaller adjoining room.

"Elin," Ryan began, his tone firm, "We have lost faith in you. Your stories don't hang together."

Raj added, "Specifically, yer dealings wi' the Defense Ministry and Takin Digital Solutions dinnae add up."

Elin, cornered and visibly distressed, attempted to defend herself, "I've been working hard, and the accounts are on track..."

Ryan interrupted her, "Elin, we've seen enough. You've missed your numbers for the last four quarters, and now you've lost our trust.. This isn't up for discussion. We can't have members on our team who aren't transparent."

Raj took a deep breath, "Elin, gather yer belongings. Ye won't be returnin' to the meetin'. We're endin' yer employment as of now. Ye'll receive three weeks o' severance pay, provided ye sign the paperwork from HR."

Elin's face turned pale, her confidence shattered. She nodded silently, trying to maintain her composure, and walked out of the room.

Returning to the main conference room, Ryan and Raj continued the meeting, but the atmosphere was now heavy with the weight of Elin's sudden departure. The incident was a sobering reminder that while ambition was essential, integrity was paramount.

CHAPTER IX

GOODMAN CANARY WHARF CHRONICLES

On the waters of London's South Dock, the aiCheckmate team assembled at Goodman Canary Wharf, a classic British chophouse with hints of a New York grill. It was a premier steakhouse known for its grass-fed Scottish beef, located on the ground floor of a tall residential condo building. It was the kind of place where business got done over steaks, handshakes, and fine wine, featuring polished mahogany doors and large glass windows looking out on the waters of the South Quay.

As Raj and Ryan entered the restaurant, the soft ambient lighting revealed a palette of deep reds and browns, creating an intimate setting. To the right was the bar with rows of finely aged wines and spirits, while the rest of the space was dedicated to neatly arranged tables adorned with crisp white linens and glistening tableware.

Ryan had instructed Raj to choose a dinner venue that featured meat. He emphasized that Raj was not to concern himself with budget. Raj fulfilled Ryan's wishes and picked Goodman based on beef sourcing. "If it's no Scottish beef, it isnae worth eatin' Mate."

Harman was a carnivore whose wife, Amy, frowned on his constant quest for the perfect New York Strip, cooked Pittsburgh-style rare. While Amy emphasized her concern for his health, Ryan felt she was more concerned about losing his income than his health and companionship. When on the road and out of Amy's watchful eye, Harman indulged himself with beef.

The sales team began filtering in, some in pairs and some alone, all wearing the remnants of the day's formal wear. They were shown to a large, reserved table at the back, a prime spot that offered a panoramic view of the restaurant and yet maintained a sense of privacy.

There was an unmistakable tension in the air, a static charge left over from the day's events. As they took their seats, there were two empty place settings, and the murmurs began. Conversations were hushed, but the name 'Elin' was mentioned enough times to make its context clear. The astonishment and confusion about her sudden absence were difficult to ignore.

Ryan, always perceptive, could sense the rising tide of whispers. As a few waiters brought out glasses of water and began pouring wine for those who wanted it, he decided to address the elephant in the room. Clearing his throat, he began, "I know many of you are wondering about Elin. All I can say right now is that certain actions have consequences, and it's a reminder for us all to maintain our integrity and transparency. Let's focus on the dinner and the road ahead."

As the sound system played Gato Barbieri's Europa, the restaurant's entrance swung open, and once again, Ryan noted, heads turned as Dee entered the restaurant. Clad in a sophisticated outfit that was form-fitting without being revealing, she had mastered the art of looking provocative yet conservative. The material clung in the right places, hinting at curves but leaving enough to the imagination. Her heels clicked softly against the wooden floor, echoing her confidence.

The entire team was caught off-guard. Mouths dropped open, and even those deep in conversation stopped mid-sentence to turn and look. There was an electric pause, an appreciative silence, as this stunning beauty whispered something into Ryan's ear and took her seat.

As the moments of surprised admiration stretched following Dee's arrival, Ryan, ever the leader, rose to his feet. "Alright, everyone, I can see that Deandra's entrance has certainly captured your attention." He grinned, trying to infuse some levity into the situation. "Allow me to introduce her."

He gestured to Dee, who stood gracefully, exuding a calm and collected demeanor. "Meet Deandra 'Dee' Volkova. Seb hired Ms Volkova's firm, Korolev Strategies. Tomorrow, she'll be laying out a comprehensive marketing strategy for our Checkmate initiative's rollout. Given the significance of this project, her insights will be crucial for our success."

Dee offered a smile, nodding in acknowledgment. "I'm excited to collaborate with such a talented group. I've been following aiCheckmate's progress and am genuinely impressed by your accomplishments and market penetration."

Ryan, seizing the moment, began introducing her to the team. "Dee, this is Lukas Müller, our expert in the German and Benelux markets." Lukas acknowledged her with a nod. "And next to him is Emma Fitzgerald, a rising star in our team."

As Ryan continued introducing her to Martina Novakova and Avi Cohen, the atmosphere gradually lightened. The team felt reenergized, the dark cloud of Elin's departure somewhat lifted by the prospect of Checkmate as an exciting new revenue generator.

Martina looked at Dee and said, "I'm looking forward to learning how to best position our products in my market," and she lifted her glass of wine towards Dee as a warm gesture of welcome.

Dee smiled and replied, "As I understand your territory, you're selling in my backyard. If you have questions that I don't have time to address during the meeting tomorrow, please contact me afterward, and I'll be happy to talk you through an individual strategy."

Michael Franks', Antonio's Song played subtly in the background, intertwining with the voices of the EMEA sales team as they made toasts, shared anecdotes, and exchanged light-hearted banter.

Avi decided to add to the festivities with a strange but true story. As the team shared stories of triumph and tall tales of exaggerated brilliance, Avi clinked his wine glass with his spoon. As everyone looked at him, he began a story. "Folks, since we're going to sell Checkmate primarily to the intelligence agencies, I'd like to share some insight into the mind of an intelligence officer."

"Years ago, when I first started in the IDF Intelligence Service, I was working with a veteran sergeant who was teaching me how to use a secure transmitter. As we were working, a disheveled lady entered our office, put an old AM radio on the sergeant's desk, and began her story."

"I have been on Earth since 1994, "she began, "and ever since I've landed on Earth, I've been monitoring foreign agents. In 1997, I uncovered a plot of Syrian agents to infiltrate our military and reported it. I stopped a plan to overthrow the prime minister in 2003; in 2007, I saved the life of the King of Jordan, and that's why you know nothing of these tragedies. Thanks to me, they never happened. Well," she continued, "today, on my radio that picks up foreign agents, I heard that this base would be under attack. As I listened to the plot, the agents sensed my presence, scarred my brain, and damaged my radio, so now it only picks up commercial radio stations and stopped picking up foreign agents. Try it, it only picks up music and news."

She continued, "So I'm here for two reasons. First, I wanted to save your lives and report the plot, and second, I was hoping you could fix my radio so it will pick up agents again."

Avi smiled as he looked around the table at his teammates and said, "I swear this is true. So this meshuga lady looks at the sergeant, and he looks her right back in the eye, and without cracking a smile, he says, 'Mam, if there are foreign agents involved, you don't want intelligence; you want counterintelligence, and they are down the hall."

And with that, the table erupted in raucous laughter while Avi added, "And that, ladies and gentlemen, is an important insight into the mindset of our target customer." More laughter, and then everyone toasted Avi.

Ryan looked around at the other diners, who were staring at the commotion emanating from his aiCheckmate team, and said, "Nice work, Avi; if we get kicked out of here for being too boisterous, that will be the first time someone other than Raj got us ejected from a classy joint."

More laughter ensued.

However, amid the cheerful clinks of glasses and bursts of laughter, an underlying current of tension pulsed between Ryan and Dee. As the team lost themselves in conversations and memories, Dee subtly pressed her leg against Ryan's under the table. The unexpected contact sent a rush of warmth up Ryan's spine, a sensation he tried to ignore.

He remembered that cold evening in Chicago: the flickering city lights, the distant hum of traffic, and a room charged with undeniable temptation. The details of that night were blurry, a fog, yet the aftermath of it lingered, weighing on his conscience like an anchor, dragging him down into a sea of remorse. While part of him yearned to indulge in the magnetic pull he felt towards Dee, another part remained anchored in the reality of his life.

His thoughts veered towards Phoebe, his vibrant and innocent daughter, who had just celebrated her tenth birthday. The image of her wide-eyed excitement as she blew out the candles juxtaposed sharply with the reality he now faced. Moreover, there was the weight of his commitment to a marriage that, though loveless, still represented years of shared experiences, struggles, and memories.

Caught in the crossfire of his desires and responsibilities, Ryan took a deep breath, silently withdrawing his leg. He met Dee's gaze briefly, seeing the flash of disappointment and understanding in her eyes. For the rest of the evening, he focused on his team, the laughter, and the stories, though the heavy weight of choices, past and impending, loomed large in the back of his mind.

Above the din, Ryan commented on Raj's fine choice of dinner venue. Raj replied, "I realized Ryan's love of steak when, during US trips 'twixt the West and East Coast, he'd insist on flyin' through O'Hare with long layovers. Why? So he could go o'er through the airport tunnel to the basement of the Hilton, home of the Gaslight Restaurant. Ach, a first-class steakhoose, but there's nae Scottish beef tae be found on the menu."

Ryan added, "It's a fine steakhouse and classy. How classy, you ask? They fill the urinals with ice, and a sign above the urinals reads, 'We hardly ever use this ice in our drinks.'"

Raj chimed in, "And Ah noticed ye always order yer bourbon at the Gaslight neat."

"I don't trust the term, hardly ever," Ryan quipped. Bringing on more laughter and more disapproving stares from the other diners.

The fine food, wine, and service of this evening provided the perfect backdrop for a team regrouping and looking forward to what lay ahead.

Ryan reflected on the day. The meeting and dinner were successful except for the Elin incident. And the specter of Dee and Ryan's conflicted feelings troubled him and occupied his mind as dinner concluded.

Part II - Queen's Pawn to D4

"Before the endgame, the Gods have placed the middle game."
— *Siegbert Tarrasch,*

CHAPTER X

THE POT GETS STIRRED

Langley, Virginia

Nestled amidst the wooded landscape of Langley, Virginia, the sprawling, discreet facility of the CIA Headquarters stood at the center of American Intelligence. Late into the night, the hum of high-powered servers provided a tranquil backdrop to the tireless work of agents and analysts alike. Yet, despite its secluded appearance, the edifice was very much connected, with digital tendrils spanning across the globe.

Anna Walsh, a top cybersecurity analyst at the CIA, was hunched over her multi-monitor setup, sifting through endless lines of code and traffic data. She'd been with the agency for over a decade after earning her Ph.D. from Carnegie Mellon in Computer Science with a concentration in Cyber Security, and few knew the CIA's digital landscape better than she did. She had always been an anomaly, a woman in a male-dominated world.

The clock read 2:03 a.m. when she felt, more than identified, something awry. Just a quick flash across one of her screens — a curious software intrusion that seemed to slip past the firewall and other security barriers. The patterns were sophisticated, not the usual script kiddie trying to make a name. Its intricacies and depth raised Anna's alarms.

She isolated the code, trying to trace its source and purpose. The speed of the intrusion and its agile maneuvers across the agency's internal networks were unlike anything she had seen before. It wasn't just bypassing firewalls; it was learning from them... adapting.

"What in the world...?" she muttered to herself.

Intriguingly, the digital signature hinted at an origin from St. Petersburg, Russia. Probably Putin's Internet Research Agency (IRA). Something about this hack sent a chill down her spine. She'd never seen anything like this before, and she'd seen it all. There was a saying in the CIA, "If Walsh hasn't seen it... it doesn't exist." Unfortunately, Anna just discovered an intrusion she'd never seen, and it most definitely existed.

With a deep breath, Anna dove deeper. She started a terminal window and began typing a series of commands, hoping to trace the intrusion's pathway. The code was moving rapidly, accessing files and copying data while leaving behind an almost imperceptible trail of breadcrumbs.

Hours passed. The untouched caramel macchiato on her desk turned cold. Anna's fingers danced across the keyboard, like a River Dance hard-shoe performer, as she tried to stay one step ahead of this digital phantom. With every hurdle she placed in its path, it would momentarily pause, only to find another way around.

By the early hours, Anna had isolated a segment of the invasive code. Running it through a virtual environment, she scrutinized its function. It was brilliant, terrifyingly so. And more than that, parts of it seemed... familiar, as if she'd seen snippets of it in some recent classified files.

Her eyes darted to a proposal binder on her shelf — aiCheckmate. She'd performed a perfunctory code review on their software during a cursory background check for a security partnership. The style of coding was eerily similar. But there was no direct connection. At least, none that she could see yet.

Her mind raced. What was the connection between this Russian-sourced intrusion and a Silicon Valley tech darling?

The night was waning, and the sun's first light began to filter through the windows. Anna, grabbing a pot of coffee from one of the burners in the kitchen, armed with a fresh pot of the Agency's rancid excuse for coffee, she sat back down. She had a mystery to unravel, one that would take her deep into the heart of a technological behemoth and across the treacherous landscape of international cyber warfare.

The game had just begun.

St. Petersburg, Russia

The Internet Research Agency (IRA) in St. Petersburg served as a covert battleground in the high-stakes ether of cyber warfare. This nondescript building appeared unassuming, but Russia's elite cyber force tirelessly worked here night and day. Doing Putin's bidding, teams of hackers toiled to tilt governments, world leaders, policies, events, and the balance of power in Russia's favor.

In a dimly lit corner of the facility, lit only by the bluish-gray light of the several monitors over which they were hunched, Alexei and Dimitri, two of the IRA's most skilled operatives, embarked on an offensive mission—their target: the secrets locked away in the heart of the CIA's digital fortress.

Weeks ago, they made a half-hearted test intrusion, which was quickly rebuffed. From the duo's perspective, this "failed" attempt was a success. Through that brief foray into the CIA's systems, they were able to determine the tools required for a successful intrusion. They requested software from their superiors, who recently supplied them with a new hacking tool from a US company.

On this day, they were toying with new hacking software provided to them by a GRU operative known only as Athena. Operating their newly purloined beta version of Checkmate software, they navigated the intricate labyrinth of cyberspace.

After their initial successful entry, their delicate digital dance through cyberspace did not go unnoticed. A faceless yet formidable adversary, armed with both skill and unwavering determination, was tirelessly countering their every move. They sparred in this silent realm of codes and algorithms, their virtual swords clashing.

Dimitri, the methodical strategist of the duo, whispered, "Whoever is on the other side of this chess match is a master. They seem to be three moves ahead of us, predicting our every move."

Suddenly, a message flashed across their screens: "I have you assholes now. Bye Bye!"

With an anguished frown, Dimitri advised Alexei, "Do not engage, Alexei; we will offer this adversary no bone on which to chew."

As they delved deeper, they accessed and began the download of a trove of classified information: codenames, covert operations, and the very essence of CIA workings. Victory seemed tantalizingly close when, without warning, data dissolved, and everything ground to a halt. The flow of data ceased, the stolen data self-imploding, and the once-welcoming doors of the system slammed shut.

Confusion clouded Alexei's face. "What just happened?"

Furrowing his brow, Dimitri swiftly attempted to reestablish their connection. "I'm not sure. It is as though the system forcibly ejected us."

"Do not worry, Dimitri; right now they have us in check, but it's not checkmate. We'll find a way to counter and aim to win the game another day.

"We will need to report this," Dimitri declared.

Together, they proceeded to the office of the IRA's leader, known only as 'The General.' Without preamble, Dimitri began, "We breached the CIA but were abruptly locked out during the extraction process."

The General raised an inquisitive eyebrow. "How?"

Alexei chimed in, "Someone on the other end detected our intrusion."

Dimitri interrupted, "After attempting countermeasures, he may have simply unplugged the systems. I'm fairly confident that no traces or digital fingerprints were left behind."

The room hung heavy with tension. The General's gaze shifted to the framed photograph of Putin on his wall, a stark reminder of the high-stakes game in which he was engaged. He did not intend to "accidentally" fall out of his fourteen-story apartment window like his predecessor. "And Checkmate? Did it perform as anticipated?"

Dimitri hesitated before responding, "Yes, until we encountered the blockage. It was surprising to both of us that our activities were detected so swiftly."

Leaning back in his chair, The General contemplated their predicament. "We must consider the possibility of an unforeseen variable. This software supplied to us is only in beta form. I was told it is not a released version. It would be prudent to halt further forays into our adversaries' systems until we possess the final version. I will ask our brothers at the GRU to ensure Athena remains close to their source. Athena has more work to do; the mission is far from complete."

Dimitri and Alexei exchanged a determined glance. The two were decorated heroes after leading the cyber operations credited with tipping the result of an American election to the benefit of Russia. They recognized that the night's setback was but a minor glitch in the vast landscape of a cyber chess match. Their careers and more, however, hung precariously in the balance, subject to their success and the capricious whims of Putin and the GRU. They realized that in Putin's Russia, success was like a Sturgeon. It didn't stay fresh very long and must be disposed of before the stench makes the air unbreathable.

Their hopes were on Athena and obtaining a more robust version of Checkmate.

7:30 AM, Langley, Virginia, USA

The secure conference room at CIA headquarters buzzed with tension. Director Rogers, flanked by senior members of the cyber division, fixed a stern gaze on the digital readouts displayed on the screen before him.

"Checkmate," he muttered, his jaw clenched in frustration.

"If our leads are correct, they've weaponized aiCheckmate's most advanced product. How did they get their hands on it? No one is supposed to have this software without our approval?"

Agent Foster, the agency's foremost expert in cyber forensics, responded with urgency, "Anna Walsh says all signs point to that, Director. The methodology, the tactics—it all screams Checkmate."

Rogers slowly shook his head and said, "If Walsh identified Checkmate, then we're going forward with her recommendations."

Screens on the wall flickered to life as intelligence leaders from the UK, Germany, France, Sweden, Israel, South Korea, Japan, Australia, and others joined the emergency meeting. The international community's cyber-security fabric felt like it was fraying.

Director Rogers didn't mince words. "We have reason to believe that an adversary has leveraged Checkmate for an intrusion. We are urging all our allies to remain vigilant and share any intel."

Moscow, Russia

Inside the imposing GRU headquarters, Colonel Ivanov carefully reviewed the latest report from the Internet Research Agency. His features remained inscrutable as he contemplated the revelations. After a few moments of silence, he picked up a secure line.

"We need to get a message to Athena and increase the urgency," he said, his voice clipped.

A voice on the other end responded with a hint of uncertainty, "Are you sure, sir? Every direct contact we make with Athena increases our chances of exposing them."

"Yes," Ivanov replied firmly. "Arrange a discreet meeting in Budapest. Two days from now."

"Understood, sir. I will inform our Agent."

No one, except the colonel and the handler on the other end of that call, truly knew who or what Athena was—a phantom in the intelligence community. Yet, the name was synonymous with power, precision, an enigma, and countless successful operations in the last dozen years.

In an undisclosed location, Athena's handler received the directive. The GRU's message was urgent, clear, and non-negotiable.

He initiated a coded message on his highly secure sat phone, the intricacies of which would baffle even the most seasoned cryptographers. The message simply read: Budapest. Two days. Usual place. Directive: Checkmate.

Stockholm, Sweden

Within the Swedish Defense Ministry, Axel Lindberg, the Head of Intelligence, occupied a historic building on Jakobs Torg in central Stockholm. The architectural blend of the old and new mirrored the nation's commitment to security and sovereignty. Inside his office, Lindberg presided over a pivotal conversation.

Hans Eriksson, Chief of Cyber Security, a tall man with a full head of silver hair and piercing blue eyes, sat across from Lindberg, his posture tense. Digital readouts flashed on the wall screens, displaying a multitude of cyber activities worldwide.

Lindberg rubbed his temples, "The Americans believe the breach is tied to aiCheckmate's Checkmate. And to think, we just began to evaluate them."

Eriksson exhaled slowly, his voice laced with concern, "Our initial assessments had given their tech a clean bill. We never anticipated this level of vulnerability, let alone its weaponization."

Lindberg leaned forward, his piercing gaze focused on the data before him. "Hans, you've been running point on this project. Who's our contact at this aiCheckmate company?"

Eriksson swiped on his tablet, bringing up a profile. "Most of our information about the product was shared with us by our friends at Langley. We haven't had any direct contact with the company, but I have a few emails from," and he checked his phone, "an Elin

Svenson. She's been hounding me for a meeting; I think she just might get what she's been after."

Lindberg barked out. "Reach out to her and set up a meeting. Don't give away too much, but in that meeting, we need to understand if she's aware of this breach and had any role in it. And, most crucially, any insights she can offer on the potential source."

The Chief of Cyber Security nodded. "I'll arrange a meeting. It's better we do this face-to-face."

The Defense Minister's voice took on a grave tone, "Tread carefully, Hans. If aiCheckmate is compromised, or worse, complicit, we might be stepping into a lion's den."

Eriksson met Lindberg's gaze with determination. "I've danced with lions before, Axel."

"Just don't come back with your shoes covered in lion shit," was Lindberg's curt reply.

As Eriksson departed, Lindberg looked out of his window, his view framed by the historic structures of Jakobs Torg and the cobblestone streets of Stockholm. The serenity of the city was juxtaposed with the storm he felt brewing in the digital ether. The next moves were critical, and Sweden's place in this vast web of cyber intrigue was about to be tested.

CHAPTER XI

CRACKS IN THE FACADE

Ryan returned to his luxurious suite at the Marriott, the echoes of laughter and camaraderie from his team dinner still fresh in his mind. He felt a sense of accomplishment and pride in his team's achievements, but as he closed the door behind him, reality came crashing back. He knew that he had thrown himself into his work, finding constant reasons... no, not reasons, but excuses, to travel, and realized the satisfaction he felt with his work and his team was a surrogate for the relationship he didn't have with Amy.

The fact that he could build, coach, mentor, and enjoy working with these people... that he had some modicum of control was a contrast to his personal life. He knew his countless hours spent at work was a coping mechanism to avoid a more significant issue. An issue that he was not going to be able to avoid much longer.

Oh, and then there was Dee; he imagined how different life could be if he had met her twenty years ago.

The dimly lit room seemed to magnify the heaviness in his heart. The muted colors of the plush furnishings created a cocoon of solitude, and he couldn't escape the looming tension that filled the air.

His phone rang, and he saw Amy's name on the caller ID. He sighed and thought, "Think of the devil," and answered, "Hey, Amy."

As he listened to her voice, frustration and resentment oozed from every word. It was a familiar dance they had been performing for years, and every step felt like he was dancing a tango down a treacherous stairway to hell. He thought if his relationship was a TV show, instead of Dancing with the Stars, he was on Dancing with the Devil. His gaze wandered out the window, the city lights painting a tapestry of distant dreams.

"Ryan, I'm sick of your traveling. I'm sick of your indifference to social status. I'm sick of your absences. Even when you're here, you're absent. And... most importantly, I'm sick of your shitty low-life job. Do you have any idea how embarrassing it is for me when all my friends' husbands are doctors and lawyers, and they ask what you do?" Amy's words pierced through the silence, and Ryan could feel his anger simmering like water in a teapot on an induction cooktop dialed up on the highest setting.

Amy felt her marriage to a "salesman" was beneath her station. Her father was a Partner in a prominent Baltimore law firm. Her friends were married to senators, lawyers, doctors, and trust fund babies. "I can't keep pretending that my husband is a respected, successful businessman," her voice squealing like feedback from a microphone on an amplifier set to eleven.

Ryan's brow furrowed as he leaned against the hotel room window. This was a conversation they'd had many times before, and it never ended well. "Amy, we've been over this. I'm good at what I do, I like what I do, and I make a decent income. If you want a lawyer in the family, go to law school."

"Not funny, Ryan," Amy's voice was an unrelenting force. "And it's not about the money. It's about social status and prestige. For instance, I want us to join the Congressional Country Club. Who is going to sponsor a used car salesman for club membership?"

"I don't golf... I don't have the patience for that crap." Ryan shot back, then sighed deeply. The Congressional Country Club was a symbol of affluence and power in their social circle, and Amy's desire to join was no secret. "Amy, we've talked about this. I don't think that the root of this recurring argument is about a country club. I don't think this is about being able to afford stuff... this is about us."

Amy's voice grew colder, "I know it's about us, Ryan. That's why I want you to start thinking about what you can do to improve my... I mean our lives."

Then, out of nowhere, the conversation took a sharp turn when Amy went in another direction... Elin Svenson. "By the way, Romeo," Amy said, her tone suspicious, "Elin called me today, asking if I knew about you and some slutty Russian marketing analyst you've been spending time with."

Ryan's blood pressure shot through the roof. He tried to contain his anger. He knew that Elin and Amy bonded during a President's Club Trip in Maui last year. He hadn't expected Elin to involve Amy in their professional relationship. "Amy, there's nothing going on between me and this analyst. Seb contracted her to work with my sales team, nothing more. Elin is simply stirring the pot out of spite. Did Elin mention we let her go today? She's just looking for a pound of my flesh."

But Amy persisted, her jealousy taking hold. "Ryan, I don't like feeling left out of your life. If you're not telling me something, it makes me wonder what else you're hiding."

Ryan's frustration bubbled up. "Amy, I've had enough of these constant accusations and fights. You don't want me in your life; you don't want or need me. All you want me to be is your butler, chauffeur, banker. And Rita's nanny teammate in Phoebe's care. We've been living this way for years now, pretending to be a happy married couple to the world for Phoebe's sake, but I think this constant bickering is doing more damage to her than staying together in a loveless marriage."

There was a heavy silence on the line, and then Amy spoke, her voice shaky, "Are you saying what I think you're saying?"

Ryan took a deep breath, his heart heavy but resolute. He'd been thinking about this for over a year now and how it would proceed. "Yes, Amy. It's time for us to face the truth. We've been drifting apart for a long time, and it's not fair to either of us. And our toxic relationship is damaging our daughter. I'm done; I'm not doing this to her anymore. I don't want her to think that what we have is a healthy relationship."

Amy shot back, "Go ahead and leave us; I'll take you for every penny you have and ever earn. Good luck having a relationship with my daughter when I'm done with you, you bastard."

"I'm not coming home," Ryan said, "I'm going to have Sandy find me an apartment and a lawyer, and she'll hire someone to pick up my things." Sandy was Ryan's assistant, a sixty-five-year-old dynamo who was efficient and loyal to a fault.

"From now on, Ryan, if you want to talk to me or Phoebe, you will have to communicate through my attorney. I know exactly who I'm going to use, and I'll do the paperwork tomorrow." Then the line went dead. Ryan stared at his phone and thought to himself - and now it begins.

As the conversation ended, it was a bitter acknowledgment of a relationship that had run its course. Ryan knew the road ahead would be difficult. He knew Amy could be vicious; she'd hire a shark of an attorney and see to it that Ryan was drawn, quartered, fileted before she sliced off his privates. And then, when it was all over, she'd sweetly say, "Bless your heart, Ryan." He had to accept the consequences. It was finally done. Perhaps, in time, it would lead to a more fulfilling life for both of them, even if it meant leaving behind the facade of their once-happy marriage.

"Well, that went well," he said to himself, "The next time I ask for a divorce, I think I'll do it over text." He needed a drink, and the hotel bar was still open.

CHAPTER XII

BONDS OF FRIENDSHIP

Avi Cohen had been Ryan's friend since high school. They ran track together, went through college together, traveled the world together, and now worked together.

The pair met in Ryan's sophomore year. Avi was a freshman at the next-door junior high school. The two schools shared athletic fields. Ryan was at track practice when he watched Avi take first place in the four hundred meters for the freshman team. Ryan walked up to Avi as the ninth-grader was hunched over in the midfield, orally emptying the contents of his stomach, making loud retching noises. The thin young man looked like he left half of his internal organs on the infield, and his loud barking sounded like he was yelling, Buick, Buick, Buick. Ryan approached the young cookie tosser, "Nice race." and asked, "What was your time?"

Avi responded in a weak, barely audible voice while wiping yellow spittle from his mouth, "Fifty-seven," which meant fifty-seven seconds, a respectable if not remarkable time for a freshman.

Ryan quipped in his characteristic, sarcastic, less than sympathetic tone, "Fifty-seven? You haven't earned the right to puke, my friend. You're not allowed to puke on my track unless you break fifty-three," he walked away, chuckling to himself.

Avi was not as impressed with Ryan as much as Ryan was with himself. A year later, Avi had his revenge when Ryan relieved his stomach full of a couple of peanut butter and jelly sandwiches consumed just before race time. Revenge is a dish best served with peanut butter.

This wasn't the opening act of your typical love story, nor the normal foundation for building a deep, meaningful, lifelong friendship. Yet, over time, Avi proved to be a swift competitor with more speed and talent than Ryan. Avi admired Ryan for his toughness and grit. Although they met under non-auspicious circumstances, the friendship developed and deepened.

The two buddies had been through a lot together. One summer break during High School, the boys embarked on an adventure-filled trip to Israel. They spent the summer using Avi's grandmother's apartment on Shlomo Ha Melekh Street in Tel Aviv as their home base. It was a time of exploration, laughter, and girls. There were times when the two boys spent hours pulling harmless pranks, sneaking into private swimming pools, avoiding police, and, of course, searching for girls.

They traveled the country, from the bustling streets of Tel Aviv to the historic sites of Jerusalem. They traveled four hours on a standing-room-only bus ride, packed in the aisles. Destination? The Sinai Desert beach resort town of Eilat. The boys couldn't find an affordable hotel room, so they slept under the stars on the beach's warm sand. The following day, they snuck into a hotel's pool locker room for a shower and got nabbed by the manager, who called the police on the two young interlopers. When they found an opportunity, they dashed off into the streets, thanking with their high school track coach, Ron Gun, for his brutal workouts that enabled them to easily flee the scene to safety.

To navigate the language difference in Israel, Avi taught Ryan phrases of little value beyond foolishness, "Yesh li et hagelida hakhi tovah," or "I have the best Ice Cream," and "ani saruff aliach, motek," meaning "I'm burning for you, baby."

Tonight was not to be one of the boy's raucous evenings. On this particular evening, the boys, now men, found themselves at the Marriot bar, Avi sipping cheap tequila while Ryan nursed a glass of Macallan 18. The dim lighting and the low hum of conversations created a comforting atmosphere.

Avi sensed something was bothering his friend, "Mana Schma?" meaning, what's up?

Ryan leaned in, his voice low, and confided to his old friend.

"Avi, you know that things with me and Amy have not been good for some time now?" Avi nodded, his eyes filled with empathy.

"They've just gotten worse. We're talking divorce, worse," Ryan's eyes moistened while his voice cracked.

Avi, his brow furrowed, placed a comforting hand on Ryan's shoulder as the two sat at the bar. "I'm sorry to hear that, my brother. That's rough. Is it that bad, there is no fixing it?"

"I don't think so. We've been trying to keep the wheels on this bus for years now. I don't think I can fix this bus, and I am pretty sure I couldn't even sell it for scrap."

"Ryan, I know I don't have to say this, but I'm here for you. I'm like Shakira, whatever, whenever, wherever. I'm here for you."

"I appreciate that, Av," Ryan sighed, sipping his bourbon. "Look, Amy and I have been drifting apart for a while now. I'm a little shaken, but I know this is for the best. I just worry about how it will affect Phoebe and my relationship with her."

"You're a good father, Ryan, and Phoebe loves you… it won't be easy, but you and Phoebe will work through this." Avi raised his glass, offering a toast. " To new beginnings, my friend. Pulling off the bandaid can be painful, but sometimes, it's the only way forward."

Ryan clinked his glass with Avi's as he tried to smile, his lip trembling some. "Thanks, Avi. You and Tali, you've got it all together. Two wonderful kids, a perfect marriage, you have what I aspired to."

Avi nodded, the lines of contentment evident on his face. "Well, nobody's life is perfect, my friend. But we work at it, and we make it work. Tali's been my rock, and I can't imagine my life without her and the kids."

Ryan nodded, his admiration for Avi's family evident. "You're lucky, Avi. You've always had your priorities straight, and you found a wonderful woman."

Avi grinned, his eyes crinkling at the corners. "You'll find your way, too, Ryan. If not with Amy, with someone who deserves you." He then had an idea, "Ryan, you have to go to Tokyo for the Asia Pac sales meeting. Why don't you save time and miles and stay with us in Herzliya before heading to Japan? It will save you the wear and tear of all that flight time, and the kids would love to see their Uncle Ryan."

As they continued to talk and reminisce about their adventures, Ryan felt a deep sense of gratitude for his friendship with Avi. At this moment, he knew he had someone he could count on, no matter what lay ahead. Bonds forged over years of shared experiences were unbreakable, and Avi's unwavering support was a reminder of the strength of their friendship.

CHAPTER XIII

MEETING ADJOURNED

It had been a good two days... business-wise. With the exception of Elin's performance and termination yesterday, Ryan was pleased with the result. Raj had built and was managing an exceptional team. Despite the routine nature of the second day, there was good energy, especially when Dee took the stage. As in Chicago, her marketing presentation seamlessly blended analytics and creativity, keeping the audience engaged.

As Dee concluded, Ryan stood and thanked Dee for her compelling work, congratulated Raj and the team on the thoughtful effort they had put in so far this year, and emphasized that they couldn't relax in the homestretch. He mentioned that everyone needs to take advantage of the game-changing Checkmate. It will revolutionize the industry. He thanked Raj for assembling a great team of professionals and organizing the meeting. He then turned to Raj, "Any last words from you, Squire Patel?"

As Ryan took his seat, the room was filled with a momentary silence, each processing the gravity of Ryan's words. Raj stood up, adjusting his Campbell of Argyll Tartan tie that accented his yellow, starched, button-down shirt and dark blue suit. He took a deep breath before addressing the team.

"Firstly, I'd like to thank Ryan for his words of encouragement and insight. It's critical for us to celebrate our achievements while recognizing the challenges and opportunities that lie ahead."

He paused, letting his gaze sweep across the room, making sure he had everyone's attention. "I've always believed that a company is only as good as its people, and looking around this room, I am filled with immense pride." In serious times, Raj's eccentric brogue mysteriously softened. "Each one of you, in your unique capacity, has contributed to our success so far. However, as Ryan rightly pointed out, we can't afford to become complacent."

Raj motioned towards the projector screen where the Checkmate product logo was displayed. "This... is our future," he proclaimed, his voice resonant. "Checkmate isn't just another product. It's a testament to our innovation, our dedication, and our unwavering commitment to leading the industry. We are on the cusp of transforming the market, and I trust each one of you to drive that change."

He concluded, "The finish line for this year might be in sight, but the race is far from over. Remember, it's not about how you start but how you finish." Then, reverting to his brogue, "Safe travels, me lads and lassies. Ye are free to return to yer homes and families."

As Raj's words settled, the room erupted in a spontaneous round of applause, a sense of camaraderie and shared purpose from every corner. The room started emptying, with most team members heading to catch their flights home. Ryan, however, wasn't in a rush; once again, he drifted to the bar.

CHAPTER XIV

AN UNEXPECTED EVENING

He sat at the bar, nursing another bourbon, and ruminated on the day; business-wise, it was a complete success. His personal life was a different matter; he felt like a failure, and his personal life was an utter disaster. Unlike Ryan's family, where his parents were married for fifty years, and his older sister, for all appearances, was happily married for twenty-four. Ryan never thought of himself as the kind of person who would give up on a commitment. He never thought he'd be the failure of his family. He toyed with the big ball ice cube in his glass, pushing it around with his finger. His thoughts were interrupted. "Hey, mind if I sit down?" There was that unmistakable scent again, her voice calm and melodious; it was Dee.

"Please do, join me."

"Everything okay? You weren't the same Ryan I've come to know in the meeting today. Something's different. You've seemed unfocused. Not the usual steely-eyed assassin." She eyed him questioningly.

Ryan hesitated, then admitted, "Things at home... get more complicated by the day. It's just been one of those days."

Dee's playful demeanor shifted to one of concern. "Well, in that case, can I buy you a drink, sailor?" she said with a wink, harkening back to their first encounter in Chicago. Ryan managed a weak smile, more of a smirk, and Dee added, "In all seriousness, how about dinner? Fancy some Indian food? There's this fantastic place not far from here."

In the short time she'd known Ryan, Dee had come to genuinely like him. He wasn't just another assignment. She admired him. He was a natural leader, charming, witty, no bullshit, and had an air about him, a gravitas that was hard to explain.

Grateful for the distraction, Ryan agreed. "Sounds like a plan."

"Great, I'm going to get out of these business clothes and take a shower. Meet you in the lobby at six?

They met in the lobby, Ryan in black jeans and a green crew-neck sweater. Dee donned a pair of high-waisted, olive green palazzo pants, giving her a breezy and casual look. Each stride revealed the hint of her tan ankle boots, the slight heel giving her a tad more stature.

She paired the pants with an ivory silk blouse. The blouse had a modest V-neck that hinted at her collarbone. The soft material draped her torso in a way that was neither too tight nor too loose, emphasizing her slender waist and complementing the wideness of her pants.

Once again, Ryan was lost in her beauty.

The weather was pleasant, so they decided to take the forty-eight-minute walk in the quiet London night air instead of squeezing into a London cab. As people walked past them, it was difficult to ignore the effect Dee had on all the passersby, men and many of the women, for that matter.

Trishna's restaurant was one of London's many fine Indian restaurants. Years ago, Chicken Tandoori had bumped Fish and Chips as the number one dish of the Londoner. The ambiance was a warm mix of traditional and contemporary. The faint aroma of spices greeted them as they settled into a cozy corner booth. Opting to trust the expertise of the waiter, they asked him to serve his favorite dishes.

Soon, their table was adorned with a colorful array of dishes: spicy chicken tikka masala, grilled to perfection; paneer makhani, a creamy concoction of soft cheese cubes drenched in a tomato-based gravy; and a variety of naans.

The food's richness was rivaled only by the depth of their conversation. Dee spoke of her impending trip to Budapest and the projects she'd been working on. Ryan mentioned he would be visiting Avi in Herzliya on his way to Tokyo. He spoke warmly about Avi and his family…they were like his family after all. Their talk drifted from work to their aspirations and dreams, and they shared moments of laughter and thoughtful pauses.

Dee thought to herself, what am I doing? Am I getting too close to this man? Am I letting my feelings interfere with my job… my mission? It had been years since she felt this way about a man, and the last time didn't end well. I must remember this is an assignment.

The check came, and Dee insisted it was hers, or more accurately, her company's turn to pay.

As they left the restaurant, the cool London breeze brushed against their faces. Somewhere between Trishna and the Marriott, their hands found each other, intertwining naturally. The gesture was simple but spoke volumes about the comfort and understanding they'd found in each other that evening. This time, he didn't shy away. This time was different. Anyone watching would assume they were lovers.

As they walked back to the hotel, they saw it looming in the distance, a silent giant against the night sky, its lighted facade blurring into the background of their consciousness. Several minutes from the hotel, it began to drizzle. The couple hardly noticed the moist air, and there was absolutely no effect on their mood. They entered the hotel, moving through the lobby in a state of suspended awareness, the world around them receding into the shadows. Their connection was a living entity, a silent symphony enveloping them in its embrace.

Almost instinctively, Ryan walked Dee to her room, their hands still entwined, the magnetic pull between them growing with each step. They stood at her door, caught in a moment of charged silence, the unspoken emotions of the day crashing around them like silent waves.

The air between them seemed to pulsate as Ryan, swept up in the whirlwind of emotions, leaned in and, without thinking, instinctively kissed her. The kiss started as a gentle exploration, a delicate dance of lips, but soon turned into a desperate melding, a silent plea, an unspoken understanding. He pulled her close, the warmth of her body a soothing balm to his tumultuous heart.

Dee, trying to push back her feelings and stay true to her mission, unlocked her door, her eyes never leaving his. She took his hand, leading him into the sanctuary of her room. The outside world ceased to exist as she closed the door, leaving a whisper of a do not disturb sign swinging gently on the knob.

Ryan awoke from a nightmare several hours later. In his dim memory of the dream, he and Phoebe were hanging on to the remnants of a sailboat that had been decimated in a squall. They were being buffeted by giant waves. Ryan became tangled in an anchor chain, which pulled him to the depths as Phoebe looked down at him through the water, her mouth open in a scream he could not hear.

Startled, he awoke and looked around the dark room, momentarily unaware of where he was. The sound of Dee's deep, steady breathing, he felt the warmth of her lying next to him on her side, her back to him. He calmed himself, moved closer to Dee, and spooned himself against her. She let out a soft sound, something between a sigh and a moan, and he fell back into a deep sleep.

CHAPTER IV

UNWINDING THREADS

Herzliya, Israel

Herzliya is a city where the ancient and the modern intertwine, showcasing contemporary boutiques amidst the backdrop of three venerable religions. The Mediterranean sun cast a luminous sheen on Herzliya's golden shores, contrasted with the persistent cadence of crashing waves. Ryan caught the scents emanating from the many eateries located at the nearby Marina, mixed with the comforting smell of sunscreen. He thought about the peace he derived from the warmth of the sun, the sound of the waves, the gulls, and all of the scents of the beach. As he lay there, he observed Avi's kids, Amos and Liat, diligently crafting a sandcastle, occasionally beckoning "Uncle Ryan" to assist. Their innocent giggles tugged at Ryan's heart, reminding him of his daughter yet offering a momentary relief from his tormented spirit.

Ryan looked out at the expanse of sand and water. "You know Avi, someday, I'm going to be a beach bum. I will live in one of the world's great beach towns, in San Sebastian, Spain, Santa Margarita, Italy, or maybe someplace in Northern Australia, where they speak a civilized language, albeit a bastardized form of it. Someday, Avi… when I retire."

As he chatted with Avi and Tali about days long gone, Ryan's mind drifted back to the events of the past two weeks. Between the high of the business summit, the implosion of his marriage, and the **mystifying** connection he'd felt with Dee, he felt more conflicted than ever. The realization that the current trajectory of his life wasn't sustainable weighed heavily on him.

"Is everything alright, my friend?" Avi's voice cut through his reverie.

The salt air and sounds of seagulls harkened back to memories, providing comfort food for the soul. With a deep sigh, Ryan shared the contours of his tangled emotions and the decisions he felt he needed to make. In the embrace of true friendship, he found the strength to map out a way forward.

Budapest, Hungary

Across the continent in Budapest, the Danube split the city into Buda and Pest. Dee, AKA Athena, sat in a dimly lit room of a discreet hotel on the Pest side, a far cry from the bustling tourist spots. The silhouette of her controller, Segei, sat across from her, face half-hidden in shadow.

The room bore the weight of Dee's turbulent past. She was born to a GRU general and Karina, an elite Russian "escort" to the Russian upper-echelon oligarchs and senior government officials. Dee resented her treatment by the state. Born into the shadows of Russia's elite yet cast aside by a father who never publicly acknowledged her, Dee's early years teetered between privilege and neglect. Dee's life was a tale of contradiction. Her mother's suspicious death when Dee was just a toddler meant she grew up without the warmth of a mother's embrace. The cold, distant acknowledgment from her father came only in the form of placement in a GRU "charm school." There, Dee was honed into the perfect asset, molding her into a seductive weapon.

Boarding school in Switzerland polished her exterior, giving her an impeccable cover and an education at Brown University further refined her worldly facade. Yet, beneath the polished veneer lay a trained operative with a single mission. By the time she was placed into Korolev Strategies, a Ukrainian company that the GRU clandestinely controlled, her skills were unparalleled. The mysterious death of Victor, a German CEO who was her third "assignment" and the only man she ever thought she could truly love, remained a dark cloud in her past. Despite her extensive training, the scars of treachery ran deep, reminding her of the looming shadow of the GRU. She vowed after that that she would suppress any emotional entanglements.

She detested Sergei. He was a pig in appearance and demeanor. Sergei's voice, cold and unyielding, brought her back. "You know what's required of you. Harman and the aiCheckmate's new software is of immense value; we need the latest version, and we have a deadline. We need to have it by the end of the month. Continue to spin Harman in your web; we need him to defect so he can help us understand how to harness the true power of Checkmate. You do this, and you will be free of us. You will be released from your service. When this assignment is completed, you will be allowed to follow your little heart wherever it takes you."

"And… what, what about Ryan, what of him and his future?", she asked, trying for self-control to calm her dread and appear emotionally uninvolved.

"You need not worry your pretty little head about Mr. Harman's future. We will see that he is dealt with once we have what we need from him."

The very thought sent a chill down Dee's spine. Her heart raced, a turmoil of dread and longing intertwining. Was this just another assignment, or had she unknowingly stepped into a world of genuine affection? She knew the answer and tried to suppress that thought, knowing that her feelings for Ryan could spell disaster for both of them. The complexity of her emotions, especially after their intimate dinner, made the task seem even more daunting. Every assignment had a toll, and this one would not be paid with spare change. The stakes kept rising.

As she left the meeting, the weight of her double life pressed heavily on her. With every step, Dee battled the conflict within, torn between duty and the budding emotions she felt for Ryan. The streets of Budapest, usually a source of solace, now seemed more like a maze, echoing her inner turmoil.

The chessboard was set, the players in motion. But as the lines between personal and professional blurred, the stakes had never been higher. As she left the meeting and walked along the cobblestone street, with the sound of a musician playing a baleful accordion, she resolved to tamp down the emotions and remain emotionally detached from her assignment. It was best to remember this is just a job, and Harman is simply an assignment. There have been men before him; there will be men in my future.

Stockholm, Sweden

Meanwhile, in the cobblestone streets of Stockholm's old town, another meeting was taking place. Directed by the Defense Intelligence Chief, his deputy Hans Eriksson found himself across a wooden table from Elin in a historic pub. Over beers and a herring sampler, Hans sipped his beer before his face turned serious. "Elin, we need to discuss Checkmate."

Elin took a sip of beer and a bite of pickled fish as she looked at Eriksson, her gaze steady. "I left the company."

Hans nodded. "So I found out, but the ministry is concerned about the software. We fear it may have been used in an attack against a friendly service. Do you have any knowledge or suspicions of how this could happen?"

Elin frowned, the weight of her own suspicions pressing on her. "I've had my concerns, especially with Ryan Harman; he's the company's Chief Revenue Officer, one of the company's first Angel Investors, and the first employee Sebastian Mitchell hired who wasn't an engineer. He's basically the number two executive in the company. Mitchell relies heavily on him. Harman knows the system as well as any of the engineers, and he has access to every line of code."

"Go on," Hans urged.

"I think he may be compromised. Harman is married, yet he's developed a relationship with a woman who claims she's Ukrainian, but I'm almost certain she's Russian. And I know that something is going on between those two. Ryan's wife and I both agree their relationship reeks more than Östermalmshallen fish market during a two-week sanitation worker strike."

Hans leaned in, his voice dropping to a whisper. "We need to keep a close eye on this. Would you help us? Can we count on you for help if needed?"

"Am I under suspicion?"

"No," he replied emphatically.

"Will I be compensated?"

"I don't know; it depends on how helpful you can be. We may be able to offer you employment if you can demonstrate your value."

Elin hesitated but eventually nodded. "Yes, I will do what you require of me."

CHAPTER XVI

UNSEEN EYES

Stockholm, Sweden

It was four-forty-five in the evening, and the land of the Midnight sun had entered its darker days. The sun had completely set, and the temperature was eight degrees Celsius, forty-six Fahrenheit. The moment Eriksson returned to the Ministry, he headed to the top floor office of Axel Lindberg, the Defense Ministry Chief of Military Intelligence. Entering unannounced and without knocking, he stood by Lindberg's desk as the Chief was wrapping up a phone call.

As he hung up the phone, Axel snapped at Hans, "What?"

"I think I've located the source of the breach," and Hans went on to recap his meeting with Elin.

When he concluded, Eriksson picked up his phone again, pressed a button on his intercom, and barked, "Get me a secure video conference line to Langley."

Langley, Virginia

At CIA Headquarters, nestled in a wooded spot between the George Washington Parkway and Chain Bridge Road, people were on high alert. After the call from Stockholm, the Counterintelligence Center was a hive of activity. Beneath the hum of overhead lights and the constant chatter of analysts was an undercurrent of concern. The Swedish Defense Ministry had dropped a bombshell. The CIA's conference room was abuzz. On the table were several quickly assembled detailed dossiers on Ryan Harman, Deandra "Dee" Volkova, Korolev Strategies, aiCheckmate, and aiCheckmate's

CEO, Sebastian "Seb" Mitchell, the fifty-three-year-old founder of the company.

Martha Kelly, Counter Intelligence Section Chief, looked around the room, "Okay, folks! Ideas! Where do we go first?"

Agent John Daniels picked up Seb Mitchell's file and said, "Seb is former NSA, he has an active Top Secret clearance, and his last poly was eight months ago. The guy is squeaky clean. I say we bring him in on this."

"Okay, that's on you, Daniels. I want him here by tomorrow afternoon," Kelly barked in her typical authoritarian and commanding manner. "I don't care if you have to put him on one of our aircraft. Here. Tomorrow… got that?"

"Yes'm," Daniels replied sharply as he and everyone else in the room clearly got her message.

Sam Barker, the Senior Analyst on the team, asked, "I have to ask, are we focusing on the real source of this shit storm? I don't think we should eliminate other possibilities." looking up from a thick dossier.

Kelly responded, "The Swedes wouldn't have contacted us if they didn't have a high level of confidence that this was legitimate. And Sam, given what you've dug up on Korolev Strategies, the shaky banking arrangements, cutouts, and phantom accounts… it's troubling."

Another agent, Farouk, chimed in, "Dee Volkova has an interesting history too; according to her dossier, she had a relationship with that German CEO of Kliedsale Aero, the German missile company. Remember, he drowned in his bathtub under suspicious circumstances a few years back? Drowned, but no water in his lungs."

Delving further into her file, he added that at Korolev, she's worked with two other global companies that later had security issues.

Martha steepled her fingers. "We need eyes on Harman

and Volkova. Assign two teams for surveillance. Monitor all communications. When Harman takes a piss, I want to know the volume, color, and PH level. I want to know everything these two do. Let's assume Volkova is one of the bad guys, and let's figure out if Harman is just her useful idiot or a traitor. And while we're at it, alert our partner agencies globally. I want everyone on the same page."

The room shifted into high gear as agents coordinated their efforts. The scope was immense: tracking two individuals across continents coordinating with global intelligence partners, all while ensuring subtlety. They couldn't spook their targets.

Herzliya, Israel

Over in Herzliya, the sun had set, and Avi's home, with its seaside view, looked picturesque. Avi's wife, Tali, prepared a meal of roast chicken spiced just right, homemade hummus, and a Mediterranean salad. Avi and Ryan did the dishes while Tali put the children to bed. Ryan had taken his laptop and sat down in the living room to read the news. It was a pleasant, relaxing evening, and Ryan, now resigned to his pending divorce, was more at peace with his home situation. The serenity was shattered when Avi's encrypted phone beeped. The alert was from an old buddy in the Mossad. The message was brief but disturbing: "aiCheckmate compromised. Harman suspected Russian collaborator with a possible Russian agent, Volkova. Beware."

Avi's heart raced. He had known Ryan for years. The very idea of Ryan betraying his country, his company, and his friends was simply meshuggah, Hebrew for crazy, but if Mossad was sending warnings, Ryan is in trouble deeper than the Dead Sea, and that means I'm in trouble... because I have no choice but to help him.

Walking into his living room, he found Ryan scrolling through his laptop, probably going through company emails. With a heavy sigh, Avi said, "Ryan, we need to talk."

Ryan looked up, sensing the gravity. "What's up, Avi?"

"Let's take a walk." Surrounded by the moon's rippling reflection and the gentle sound of the waves, they walked until they knew there was no one within a hundred yards of them. In a hushed voice, Avi said, "Israeli intelligence has flagged you and aiCheckmate. They believe Dee is a Russian agent, and you handed her the new Checkmate software."

Ryan's face went pale; his stomach dropped so low he almost looked down at the sandy beach to see if he left his stomach there. "Are you shitting me? How do you know this?

"A buddy from my old unit, now with the Mossad. I'm as tight with him as I am with you. He knows I work for you, and he's worried for me. He took a big risk by messaging me."

"Avi, this is ridiculous! I would never betray my country. I don't know any Russians and," he stopped and thought about Dee, the "Ukrainian." As his mind raced, he flashed back to the night he met her… the open laptop…. all those so-called chance meetings, "Damn!"

"I believe you, Ryan," Avi said, his voice firm but sympathetic. "But I may be the only one who believes you. Multiple agencies are onto this; we're not just talking about a business mishap. This is global espionage, sabotage, and cyber terrorism. This is dangerous. Really dangerous."

Ryan swallowed hard, processing the weight of it all. He had sensed Dee was more than she seemed, but to be caught in an international intelligence crossfire was beyond his wildest imagination.

The two men looked at each other, realizing they were now in uncharted waters, boiling uncharted waters, and if not now, soon there would be unseen eyes watching their every move. It was time for a plan.

CHAPTER XVII

THE GAMES BEGIN

Langley, Virginia

Martha Kelly, the seasoned chief of the counterintelligence section at the CIA, sat in her office with Sebastian "Seb" Mitchell, formerly of the National Security Agency and now the Founder and CEO of aiCheckmate. Seb was an engineering-oriented CEO who was the chief architect of the product and very hands-on in its development. The air in the room was tense, charged with an urgency that couldn't be denied.

Mitchell, a man with a reputation for his brilliance in the world of cybersecurity, leaned forward, his brows furrowed with curiosity. "Okay, I'm here. Where's the fire?" he asked, his eyes fixed on Kelly.

Kelly wasted no time; she dropped a file in front of him, her expression grave. "We have strict export rules over your Checkmate software. So, how did it get into the hands of the Internet Research Agency? They weren't on our approved list, were they?" She added sarcastically.

Mitchell shuddered, feeling a prickling sensation on the nape of his neck. His once firm resolve began to falter, sensing the weight of the moment. "Hold on, Madam, I'm not comfortable with your insinuation."

Kelly leaned back in her chair, her gaze unwavering. "I'm not implying anything, Seb. I've talked to your former supervisors at The Fort," she said, referencing the NSA headquarters at Fort Meade, Maryland. "They assure me you are beyond reproach. What I'm about to share with you is for your eyes only."

With that, Mitchell reviewed the file in front of him. The document detailed the recent cyberattack on the CIA and provided evidence that left no doubt: the Russians had used Checkmate, Mitchell's software, in their breach.

Mitchell's eyes widened as he scanned the report. "How did this happen?" he asked, his voice tinged with a mix of disbelief and concern.

Kelly's response was concise and direct. "That's why we summoned you here, Seb. We need to find out how your software ended up in their hands. We suspect that your own man, Ryan Harman, facilitated the leak. We want to know if he was careless, stupid, or if he's an enemy of the state."

Mitchell ran a hand through his hair, his mind racing. "I trust Ryan, or at least I thought I trusted him," he began, his words measured. "I don't believe he's capable of that kind of betrayal, but I can't vouch for him. Do you want me to call him..."

Kelly interrupted him with a stern look. "No, Seb. Don't call Ryan. We can't afford to tip our hand just yet. Let no one know about the breach. Just tell us what you know about the software, what this breach report tells you, and how you think they could have gotten their hands on your code. Most importantly, tell us how to protect ourselves from Checkmate."

"How do we protect ourselves? The only guarantee of that is to take every computer in the world off the net," was his off-the-cuff reply.

Mitchell leaned back, deep in thought. After a moment, he began to outline some of his theories, from the unlikely act that his internal systems were hacked to there being a traitor in his company. Each theory was more troubling than the last. As he spoke, the weight of the situation settled in the room, and both he and Kelly understood that they were facing a threat that could have far-reaching consequences.

Mitchell looked at Kelly, "I'm afraid that there is nothing that can stop Checkmate if it falls into the wrong hands. A party with evil intent could destroy every networked computer on Earth. You can't stop Checkmate; you have to take it away from the bad guys or take the bad guys away from it."

Seb rested his hand on his forehead, a look of despair on his face as he paraphrased Robert Oppenheimer, the director of the Manhattan Project, "I'm afraid that I have become death, destroyer of cyber worlds."

Herzliya, Israel

Ryan woke in Avi's guest room, the soft sunlight filtering through the sheer curtains. Despite the anxiety he felt the night before, he woke with a clear mind and heart, determined to get through this ordeal. The comforting aroma of freshly brewed coffee wafted through the air, melding with the distant sounds of children's chatter.

Stretching his limbs, he got up from bed and dressed quickly. As he stepped into the kitchen, Tali greeted him with a warm smile and a steaming hot cup of freshly brewed coffee. Before he could react, she leaned in, planting a chaste, sisterly kiss on his forehead.

"Manishma?" she asked with genuine concern in her eyes.

"Tov, beseder," he replied, exhausting his practical Hebrew. He knew Tali was a polyglot, fluent in four languages, which reminded him of the old joke, "You know what you call someone who speaks one language? American." Ryan was decidedly an American.

With a motherly gesture, Tali pointed to a steaming plate on the dining table. "Avi had already eaten. Sit... eat," the former Israeli Defense Forces sergeant ordered in her accented English.

Recognizing the dish, Ryan's mouth watered at the sight of the shakshuka - a fragrant mixture of poached eggs in a spicy tomato and pepper sauce. As he took his seat, the sounds of footsteps grew louder, and Avi's two children burst into the kitchen, their faces lit with joy.

Tali gently prodded them, "Give Uncle Ryan a kiss. Abba is driving him to the Airport. He's off to Japan, so he won't be here when you return from school."

Without hesitation, the kids ran to Ryan, wrapping their small arms around him in a warm embrace. "Shalom," they chirped in unison, their voices sweet and melodious.

As Tali escorted the children out of the house to walk them to school, Avi entered the kitchen. His face was stoic, betraying no emotion, but his eyes spoke volumes. Without uttering a word, he placed a finger to his lips, signaling Ryan to remain silent. He then carefully placed a note on the table.

"Watch what you say. My former associates may be listening.".

Ryan took a moment to process the warning; he felt a sudden chill, his appetite suddenly diminished. He was reminded that he was now playing a higher stakes game than simply competing to exceed a quota. He finished his meal quickly and stood up, ready to face the next challenge.

The two men entered Avi's car, a beat-up, dented, black Jeep Cherokee, and exited Cohen's driveway. Avi, an experienced former intel officer, kept checking his rearview mirrors, ever alert for a tail. Ryan took no notice of his friend's vigilance. Unlike Avi, he was a neophyte in the dangerous chess match in which he was now innocently embroiled.

Fifteen minutes after leaving his neighborhood, Avi spotted the tail in a dark blue Peugeot. He was gravely concerned for his friend, who had no intelligence, surveillance, or evasion experience. Was Ryan up for this dangerous game?

As they entered the highway, Avi smirked, "Off to Lod airport then."

Ryan raised an eyebrow, "You mean Ben Gurion?"

Avi chuckled, "You call Reagan National, National Airport because that was its name for fifty years before they added Ronny to the moniker. We locals have our ways." Avi's forced levity was intended for any listening devices that may have been surreptitiously placed in the car.

Ryan thought, "Certain things feel too ingrained to change, no matter the official titles or the passage of time. The two friends meant no disrespect to the namesakes of those two airports. Just like New Yorkers who refuse to call Sixth Avenue, Avenue of the Americas meant no disrespect to America.

Avi stopped at the Egyptair terminal; Ryan would have a layover in Cairo on his way to Narita Airport. As Ryan went to the trunk to grab his luggage, Avi joined him, giving him a warm hug as he surreptitiously slipped something into Ryan's windbreaker pocket. With purpose in his step, Ryan walked off to the check-in counter.

Unnoticed by Ryan, Avi confirmed that the dark blue car was stopped three cars behind them. This was the vehicle that had followed the pair since they left Avi's neighborhood. He watched his old friend walk into the terminal and noticed a passenger leave the Peugeot and follow Ryan into the Egyptair arrival doors. Not an overly religious man, Avi said a prayer, thinking to himself, "Go with god, my friend. You can use all the help he can get."

Budapest, Hungary

After a long, restless night, the morning in Budapest finally arrived, painting the city in a golden hue. The Corinthia Hotel, a grand old dame, stood proudly amidst the cobblestone streets, its neoclassical façade paying homage to a bygone era. Built-in the 1800s, the hotel oozed old-world charm, starkly contrasting with the modern opulence within its walls. Majestic chandeliers hung from the ceilings, casting soft, luminous glows, while plush carpets cushioned every step. Dee slowly stirred in the luxurious suite, the warmth of high-thread-count sheets wrapped around her.

But the grandeur around her did little to comfort Dee. Beside her, Sergei, her Russian handler, lay snoring; his stinking breath assaulted her, every guttural sound magnifying her disdain. This pig was the embodiment of the dominion her Russian masters held over her: expecting her to serve their political strategies and fulfill their lecherous desires. As she glanced at his oblivious face, she wished, for a brief moment, that his peaceful slumber would extend into eternity.

The night's rest had done her no favors. Tossing and turning, her mind raced with the thoughts of Ryan Harman. There was a sincerity about him that made her heart waver. But with Sergei's warning echoing in her mind, her hopes of a possible life with Ryan seemed a distant dream. Memories of Victor flooded her thoughts, and she felt an icy grip of fear. Could Ryan meet the same dark end? She thought to herself, would Ryan sacrifice himself for me? I need to take care of myself first and not let sentimentalities get in the way.

Dee quietly rose from the bed to avoid waking her tormentor, determined to find solace, if only for a day. With the grandeur of the Corinthia behind her, she decided on a place that might offer her some calm: the City's Beer Thermal Spa. The Budapest subway took her through the city's heart, where old and new architectures intertwined, narrating tales of histories and futures.

The spa was an oasis amidst the urban sprawl. Warm, therapeutic waters welcomed visitors into their embrace, the mineral-rich composition promising healing. For centuries, these thermal baths had been the go-to for the weary and the wounded. Dee, donning a swimsuit, submerged herself into the amber liquid, its effervescence caressing her skin. It was said that the beer ingredients - malt, hops, and yeast- and the thermal waters- had revitalizing properties. She closed her eyes, allowing the bubbles to envelop her, wishing they could wash away the dread that lingered in her heart. Could she ever truly escape the clutches of her Russian overlords?

Unbeknownst to Dee, her every move was being shadowed. Not far from the spa's entrance, the subtle movements of a CIA surveillance team went unnoticed. They monitored her closely as she enjoyed a false sense of solitude, soaking in the healing water where she sought refuge.

The serene surroundings of Budapest stood in stark contrast to the storm brewing in her life.

CHAPTER XVIII

FIGHT OR FLIGHT

Twenty-five-thousand feet in the air somewhere over the Sinai

As Ryan settled into his plush Business Class seat aboard Egyptair, he couldn't help but feel a sense of unease. The past few weeks had been a whirlwind of activity, a melange of business, personal, and now espionage. He reached into his pocket and found a burner phone, put there by Avi, a reminder that events beyond his control had him walking a dangerous path. The note instructed him to purchase a SIM card upon landing in Cairo and make the calls they had discussed, but even this seemingly simple task carried a weight of uncertainty. Could he depend on the small list of people critical for his success to come through?

He opted to stay in Cairo for the next two nights. Believing that a moving target is more challenging to hit, he was reluctant to remain in one location for too long. A brief stopover in Cairo would allow him to have things in place when he arrived in Japan.

The airplane's engines roared to life, signaling the beginning of their short hour-and-a-half flight. Ryan leaned back in the comfortable seat, the soft hum of the cabin providing a momentary respite from the chaos that had consumed his life. With the steady hum of the engines in the background, he took a deep breath and began to reflect on the events that had led him to this point.

Phoebe. He hadn't spoken to her since leaving for London, and the guilt weighed heavily on him. She was the one person he needed to protect from this growing, dangerous affair. He wondered if Amy was poisoning Phoebe against him. A pang of longing mixed with worry washed over him, but there was no time to dwell on it now.

Amy, on the other hand, was a different matter entirely. She had distanced herself from him, refusing to answer his calls, which cut off all contact with his daughter. He knew her well enough to be certain that she had sought the best lawyer in town, and that lawyer was likely preparing to unleash a legal storm that would leave him battered and broken.

Amy, never one to find fault in her actions, would be determined to make him pay for their deteriorated relationship. Everything in her mind that was wrong with their life was Ryan's fault, but now, this time, maybe she would be right. She'll be out for blood, and Ryan could hardly blame her.

Unbeknownst to Ryan, hidden in the shadows of the airplane's cabin were members of a CIA surveillance team. They had been tracking his every move, ensuring that their target did not slip away. Meanwhile, another operative waited patiently at the gate, ready to take over the surveillance once Ryan disembarked in Cairo.

As the flight attendant approached, Ryan was momentarily pulled from his thoughts. She was an efficient, poised woman, her uniform impeccably neat. Her name tag read Aya, and she greeted him with a warm smile.

"Good evening, sir," Aya said, her voice tinged with a hint of a British accent. "Is there anything I can get you before we take off?"

Ryan cleared his throat, torn between his thoughts and the present moment. "Yes, actually," he replied, thinking to himself, I could use a pint of bourbon, but instead forcing a small smile, he said, "Just a black coffee, please."

She nodded, making a note of his request. "Of course, sir. I'll have that brought to you shortly."

As she walked away, Ryan's mind continued to race. The burner phone and Avi's instructions weighed heavily in his pocket, a reminder that his journey was far from over. With the looming uncertainty of what lay ahead, he couldn't afford to let his guard down, not even for a moment. The plane taxied down the runway, and as it took off into the night sky, Ryan's fate remained entwined with the secrets and dangers that awaited him in Cairo.

Budapest, Hungary

Dee, now dressed and rejuvenated after her spa visit, left the serene atmosphere behind and stepped out into the bustling streets of Budapest. She was a highly trained professional skilled in the art of espionage and evasion. It didn't take her long to spot the surveillance team tailing her. The question that burned in her mind was whether they were Russian operatives or part of some other intelligence service.

She decided to play a little game, a cat-and-mouse chase through the historic streets of the city. Dee casually strolled to a nearby hop-on-hop-off bus stop and boarded the double-decker tourist bus. Her pursuers followed, discreetly taking seats on the upper deck.

She exited the bus in the vibrant heart of Budapest's Great Market Hall. Dee reasoned that the crowds and rows of stalls would give her a chance to test the mettle of her pursuers and analyze their methods. Dee entered the market beneath its ornate steel framework and the colorful Zsolnay tiles. She was surrounded by locals and tourists alike as they bustled about, shopping for fresh produce, spices, meats, and souvenirs. Dee took her time, wandering and inspecting stalls, her movements making surveillance difficult.

Her hands gracefully maneuvered through displays of ripe tomatoes and fragrant herbs, occasionally resting on the small leather crossbody bag she wore for her outing at the baths.

As she neared the food stalls on the upper floor, the tantalizing aroma of Hungarian cuisine enveloped her. Stall owners called out, advertising their delicacies, from gulyás to lángos. She stopped in front of a vendor selling freshly made pörkölt, a rich and hearty stew served over nokedli, little dumplings similar to German Spätzle.

With a quick exchange of forints, she was handed a steaming bowl.

She had taken the measure of her uninvited surveillance team, and as she finished her stew, she rapidly exited the market and she once again hopped on the Hop-On-Hop-Off bus.

This time, Dee disembarked at the iconic Chain Bridge, a breathtaking structure spanning the Danube River. She walked the length of the bridge, admiring the view of Budapest illuminated in the evening light, all the while covertly evaluating the spy craft of her shadows. Their movements, their body language—it all held clues to their true allegiance. "This is not Russian spycraft. Who are they, and what do they want from me," she asked herself.

Convinced that the surveillance team was American, Dee continued her strategic escape. She made her way to the funicular that led to Buda Castle. The historic funicular was a popular tourist attraction, and she knew the crowds would offer her cover.

Inside the Citadella, the hilltop fortress swarmed with tourists. Dee blended in, carefully weaving through the throngs of people. Her destination was a church nestled among the historical buildings. As a group of women entered the church, she seized her opportunity. Without drawing attention, she slipped into a busy women's restroom and found solace in a stall.

Fortunately, Dee had planned for contingencies. She retrieved a change of clothes from the bag she had brought to the spa. In her new attire, she exited the stall and approached two women, one wearing a scarf. In a hurried but hushed tone, she explained that an old boyfriend was stalking her and pleaded for their assistance.

Her request was met with sympathetic nods, and one of the women offered Dee a jacket and scarf to conceal her identity further. With her newly acquired allies by her side, they exited the church, arms on arm, blending into the crowd of oblivious tourists. The surveillance team had lost their target.

Once safely out of sight, Dee made a call to her controller, Sergei. She requested that he meet her at the train station with her passport and a ticket to Vienna. Time was of the essence, and the next leg of her journey held its own set of challenges and dangers. Dee had mastered the art of eluding those who pursued her, but she knew that each step meant new vulnerabilities and danger.

Herzliya, Israel - Virginia Waters, United Kingdom

Ten minutes after dropping off Ryan, Avi quickly dialed Raj's number. Ryan and Raj's connection was more than just business. Avi knew that Ryan's trust in Raj was warranted. Like Avi, this quirky Scottish Indian was someone Ryan could rely on.

At his home in Virginia Waters, a picturesque and affluent London bedroom community in Surrey, England, Raj's phone rang. Raj lived in an elegant, sprawling mansion that was luxurious and charming. The house was nestled amidst lush greenery, surrounded by tall trees that provided a sense of seclusion and tranquility.

Raj looked at the caller ID and noted it was Avi. Raj answered, "What's up, Avi?"

Avi relayed a message that would not alert anyone listening to the true purpose of the call. He needed to make sure that Raj would pick up Ryan's call from an unknown number. "Raj," Avi began in a serious and urgent tone, "in the next two hours, you should expect a call from one of my prospects. This is a critical call. The prospect is seeking pricing concessions that I don't have the authority to approve. The call will be from my decision maker, Amr Abdelrahman, from Vodafone Egypt. Please, if you get a call with an Egyptian country code... answer it."

Raj nodded on the other end of the line, "No worries, Avi," he assured his colleague, "The Vodafone business is critical to making our numbers this year; I'll be on the lookout for a call from Egypt."

Cairo International Airport, Egypt - Virginia Waters, United Kingdom

Hurrying off the plane, Ryan found a kiosk selling cheap mobile phones, earbuds, portable phone batteries, and SIM cards. He purchased a SIM card and found a relatively quiet corner to perch where he had an excellent view of his surroundings. He quickly dialed Raj's number.

Raj's phone rang; he saw that it read plus twenty, the Egyptian phone country code, and thought, here's the Vodafone guy Avi told me about. He answered, "Raj Patel, aiCheckmate," he was taken aback when he heard Ryan's voice.

"Look, Raj, I have to make this quick. I'm in trouble, like real trouble. You are going to hear things about me. Trust me, buddy, I did nothing wrong. I'm going to ask you to do some favors for me, but before I do, I need to let you know that what I'm asking could get you in trouble, like prison-time trouble."

Raj's jaw dropped; this sounded scary, but there was no question he and Ryan were members of the same clan, and he knew that Ryan wouldn't ask him to do anything that Ryan wouldn't do for him. Without hesitation, he said, "Whatever you need from me, whatever the consequences, I'll do everything in my power that you ask. Damn the consequences,"

"I have a quick list. Remember that white hat hacker you told me was part of Anonymous? You know that guy in London we used for our pen test on the initial product?"

A "pen test" is short for "penetration test." It is a cybersecurity assessment and testing process to identify vulnerabilities and weaknesses in a computer system and network. Penetration testers, often referred to as ethical hackers, conduct these tests to simulate real-world cyberattacks and assess the system's resilience against various threats.

"Sure, Ryan, you mean Eddie. He's the best."

"Well, I need you to contact him, get him to write some code for me. Pay whatever he asks, and I'll get the money back to you."

Raj interrupted, "I'm not worried about the stupid money, mate. What else?"

"I need him to give it to you on a thumb drive and then bring it to our meeting in Tokyo. Don't spend time saving me money; pay what he asks." Ryan then detailed a list of functional requirements for the software code.

"Next, I need you to call Dex Johnson. You know him; he's the ex-Marine, New England sales guy based in Boston. I need you to get him to call me at this number within the next forty-five minutes. Swear him to secrecy; he can tell no one about the call. I trust him. Not like I do you or Avi, but he's good people. After you talk to Dex, don't talk about this to anyone. When you talk to Avi, keep it strictly business. This conversation never happened. I'm afraid that people are listening to Avi's calls, and before too long, they may be listening in on yours."

"You got it, Ryan... I'm on it."

Marblehead, Massachusetts - Cairo International Airport, Egypt

Ryan's phone rang, and he could see by the caller ID that it was Dex. "Hi, Dex, I need your help, and I need you not to ask any questions. All I can tell you is that I'm in trouble. I haven't done anything wrong, and I need your help."

"What do you need, boss?"

"When you were interviewing for this job, you told me you were considering working with your Marine buddies from Afghanistan to join their private protection company. I need to hire them. I'm going to need four of their best people for a month. I can't pay upfront, so I need you to convince them to share the risk with me. I'll pay them three million dollars if they keep me alive for a month. If they fail, they can send my bill to the morgue. If you can get them to agree, I need them to meet me in Tokyo at the Grand Prince Hotel Takanawa in two days."

Dex felt the old adrenaline as if he was going into battle. He replied, "You got it, Boss. Anything I can do? You want me there too?"

"I appreciate that, Dex. I'd love to have you there, but it would complicate things. I'll explain later. Now, forget we ever had this call, and I owe you, Dex."

"No, Boss, you've done plenty for me. I will see you again, and if I don't, it's been a pleasure serving with you, sir."

"Don't call me sir; I work for a living." Ryan hung up, turned off the phone, took out the SIM card, and walked to the exit where he could find the hotel shuttles. He would destroy the phone and SIM card as soon as he could dump them unobserved.

He quickly stepped towards the exit to pick up his shuttle to the Novotel Airport Hotel, where he would spend the next two days, holed up in his room while testing the quality of the hotel's room service.

He didn't notice the CIA operative who helplessly watched Ryan make the calls and thought to himself, "What the hell was that about? I wish I had learned to read lips."

CHAPTER XIX

PLAN TO ACTION

South Boston, Massachusetts

Across the Atlantic, at Shea's Tavern, located on Broadway in South Boston, Dex met with Roger, "The Dodger" Scranton. The two were old Marine Corps buddies. Scranton was the founding CEO of Sentinel Shield—a prestigious private security firm whose tagline "Guarding Tomorrow Today" resonated with its commitment. The two men were seated in a booth, chugging Budweisers and trading war stories.

Then Dex got down to business, "Look, Rog, I need your help."

"Anything you need, Dex, you know that. Look, brother, we've been through hell together, and you've pulled me out of the shit more than once. What do you need?"

"That's the thing, this isn't for me. It's for my boss. This guy is more than just my boss; he's been a big help to me as I've transitioned from the Service to civilian life. And, Rog, I feel like he's one of us. You know what I mean? He's a good egg who'd have our back in a firefight."

Dex described the seriousness of Ryan's situation, detailing the kind of personnel he had in mind for the security detail. Provided they kept their client alive, the money was generous. After Dex hashed out the requirements, Roger mentally scrolled through his extensive roster of skilled operatives. He'd go back to his office, figure out who was available, and ensure he assembled a team with the right mix of skills and the chemistry to work together under pressure.

"I'll have the team assembled and ready to go in twenty-four hours," Scranton assured Dex. Scranton got up from the table, put his hand on Dex's shoulder, looked him squarely in the eye and said, "Don't you worry, Dex, I will protect your guy like he's my brother. And unlike you, I like my brother."

Bedford, Massachusetts

Roger got to work, meticulously coordinating every detail. In his corner office at Sentinel Headquarters, he sorted through dossiers, finally landing on four highly experienced professionals. For the team lead, he chose Derek Garner, a former captain in the special forces, who had been with Sentinel for eleven years and led over two dozen successful assignments. At five foot eight and one hundred and sixty-five pounds, he was deceptively powerful. Garner was a natural leader with an extraordinary combination of high IQ and EQ. He was fast-thinking and decisive, and men would follow him through titanium-reinforced brick walls.

Next, he chose the inappropriately named Jake Little. Jake stood six foot two and was two-hundred-and-twenty pounds of pure muscle and sinew. His list of competencies included electronics, electronic countermeasures, and surveillance.

Scranton needed a Russian speaker, and for that role, he selected Richard Kurtz. Kurtz's parents were Russian immigrants, and he learned Russian before picking up English. He was a former Army Ranger and an excellent marksman.

To round out the team, he chose Phil Eichel. Eichel was a gentle giant who dwarfed even Jake Little. He was a six-foot-four gym rat whose muscles had muscles—an Alabama boy with a charming, soft-spoken southern drawl and a gentle nature. Yet, when challenged, Phil could and had dispatched would-be assailants to emergency rooms throughout the globe. He would serve as muscle and driver.

Scranton then arranged accommodations at Tokyo's Takanawa Prince Hotel, ensuring they would be strategically positioned in rooms adjoining Ryan's. Every angle was considered, and every potential threat was anticipated. They were not just protecting a client; they were safeguarding someone who was extremely important to a fellow brother-in-arms.

Cairo International Airport, Egypt

Forty-eight hours later, as the shimmering afternoon sun pierced through the colossal windows of Cairo International Airport, casting elongated shadows on the polished marble floors. The rhythmic hum of distant announcements, punctuated by the hurried footsteps of passengers, created an atmosphere of restless energy. Amidst the crowd, Ryan moved with purpose and discretion. Every step was measured, and each glance calculated. Through the windows he could see the Mokattam hills in the distance, but he remained oblivious to the eyes that trailed him. Those eyes belonged to seasoned CIA operatives, trained to merge seamlessly into the background.

Vienna International Airport, Austria

In the grandeur of Vienna International Airport, the modern elegance of Baroque and contemporary design stood in stark contrast to the opulent grandeur of the city's thirteenth-century old town. Dee, satisfied that she was not being followed, settled into the plush embrace of her seat on a KLM flight. Her departure from the city of music and dreams, the former home of Mozart, Beethoven, and Schubert, signaled the next movement in a dramatic symphony that would unfold in Tokyo.

London, United Kingdom

Thousands of miles away in the rain-soaked streets of the Peckam neighborhood of London, Raj sat in the dimly lit underground office of the master hacker. The room was filled with the gentle whir of computers and the faint blue light of multiple screens. He was deep in negotiations with Eddie, who was allegedly affiliated with Anonymous. Years ago, aiCheckmate contracted with this bespectacled diminutive computer geek to pen test the company's early product.

As Raj relayed Ryan's intricate software specifications, the hacker's fingers danced over the keyboard. Eddie, motivated by accomplishing unaccomplishable cyber hacks, would do this simply for the sport of it, but he asked for twenty thousand pounds. Two hours later, Eddie handed Raj a thumb drive, and Raj was ready for his trip to Tokyo.

Narita Airport, Japan

Tokyo's skyline, a mesmerizing mix of ancient temples and soaring skyscrapers, loomed in the distance as Ryan's plane touched down. His internal debate about the train journey from Narita was both practical and emotional. Memories of a past lengthy delay caused by a tragic incident when a disgraced CEO from a local electronics company resigned by kissing a locomotive instead of handing in a simple resignation letter. Decision made, Ryan chose the familiar comfort of a taxi, foregoing the possible drama of another unscheduled corporate resignation and train delay. He remained unaware of the choreographed switch of agents shadowing him.

Tokyo, Japan

Not long after Ryan's plane landed, Dee arrived at the hotel alone after successfully ditching her tail back in Budapest. As she navigated the opulent lobby, a seemingly inconspicuous Asian woman engrossed in a newspaper discreetly observed her every move. The woman checked at the desk, returned to her chair, and spoke into her lapel, "She's arrived and is in room eight-two-three, repeat, eight-two-three."

Her headpiece crackled, "Roger that."

Moments later, Ryan arrived at the hotel, once in his room, he checked his watch and saw that it was nearly six o'clock. Raj would be arriving any minute. Ryan headed to the Club Lounge and took a seat at the bar. The attendant asked him for his order; Ryan said, "Tozai Sake, please," and bowed his head to the bartender; then he thought, I need something stronger and quickly added, "I'm sorry, please change that to Iichiko Shochu, neat."

Moments later, Dee rolled into the bar. Ryan thought she was like the tides; you could depend on her to roll out and back in again. Although, unlike the tides, her timing was not quite as predictable. She cozied up to Ryan. "We really need to stop meeting like this," she said as she put an arm around him, kissed him gently on the cheek, and added, "What are you drinking?"

This woman betrayed him. Feeling a confusing mix of intense anger and lustful desire, Ryan, who had never really been good at hiding the quality of his hand at Poker, tried to display the unemotional masked face of a professional gambler. Concealing his anger, he smiled and replied, "I'm having Shochu. Great to see you," and then added, "Dee. I missed you." At that moment, he missed her like a slug missed a salt shaker. But he hoped his face said he missed her like a heart that missed its beat.

Dee motioned to the bartender and, in perfect Japanese, asked for the same drink as Ryan.

Fifteen minutes later, Raj entered the lounge, jovial as ever; he stood behind both Dee and Ryan, with his hand on their backs, and said, "Ah, a warm welcome to ye! May yer days be as long and satisfying as a Scottish summer's eve, and may yer heart be as full as a pub on a Saturday night!"

Ryan looked at Dee and said, "Dee, Raj, and I need to review our plan for tomorrow's meeting. I really want to spend time with you, but this is critical. We can catch up tomorrow after the meeting. Okay?"

Dee looked hurt. Not wanting to tip her that he knew she had betrayed him, Ryan added, "Really, tomorrow, you can join the group after dinner, like we did in London, and then you and I can spend quality time together after dinner. Look, Dee, I miss you like the desert misses rain. But you must understand, I have responsibilities. Now, if you'll excuse us." With that, he gave her an affectionate kiss.

Ryan and Raj walked over to a private table and discussed the planning for tomorrow's account reviews and the upcoming meeting. There was no mention of the recent intrigue. Both assumed the walls had ears, the tables had ears, and the people in the lounge with ears had ears. As they left to retire for the evening, Raj shook Ryan's hand and clandestinely passed the thumb drive to his boss and friend.

CHAPTER XX

LAYERS OF SECURITY

The evening air in the hallway of the Takanawa Prince Hotel was still, undisturbed by the soft padding of Raj and Ryan's footsteps as they headed to their respective suites. Each room's door clicked shut with an air of finality, signaling the end of their shared discussions for the day.

He pushed open the door to his room, the dim ambient light briefly framed Ryan's silhouette before he stepped into the muted luxury of his room. He hesitated for only a moment before approaching one of the two inconspicuous doors connecting his suite to the adjoining rooms. With a quiet turn of the handle, the door creaked open to reveal the vigilant gaze of the Sentinel Shield security team.

Their hushed greeting, a mix of respect and camaraderie, filled the room as Ryan pulled the door shut behind him. The leader, a compact, black man with piercing hazel eyes, nodded toward him, his eyes holding a wealth of experience and an unspoken promise of protection. "We'll need to run a standard sweep for any listening devices. Our first priority is to make sure private stays private," he murmured.

One of the men, wearing a sleek dark suit, quickly moved into action. With a strategic swiftness, he turned on the television, letting the droning voice of the BBC News anchor fill the room. Following that, the shower's cascading water masked any residual sound. Only then did he start his meticulous sweep of the room, systematically scanning each corner, every possible hiding spot. A brief nod signaled the discovery and removal of bugs from various locations: the phone, the underbelly of the bathroom vanity, and a couple more unsuspected places.

As the bugs were placed on the table, Ryan's voice broke through the mechanical hum of the television. "There's going to be a lady joining me either tonight or tomorrow. I need absolute assurance that no one enters or approaches the room and that the team monitors the conversation. I'm not one hundred percent sure if this lady is friend or foe. I'm leaning towards foe, and I'm concerned she may bring company."

Jake, a Sentinel operative who was designated to reconnoiter the hotel and identify Ryan's unwanted babysitters, nodded, Jake's years of training and experience imbued him with the ability to recognize the patterns of covert surveillance, to sense the presence of those who hid in plain sight. His perception was finely tuned, his nerves trained to pick up subtle cues – a lingering glance, an awkward stance, or a quiet radio check. His mission was clear: "I'll identify anyone watching you from the shadows and neutralize them.

Ryan's brow furrowed as he processed their plan. "Neutralize? What exactly do you mean by that?"

The leader, who introduced himself as Captain Derek Garner, leaned in slightly, carefully choosing his words. "Neutralize, in our context, doesn't imply lethal force. If we identify any threats, our priority will be to immobilize them temporarily—enough to ensure your safety without causing lasting harm."

Ryan nodded, the tension in his shoulders relaxing slightly. "I need to make sure that no harm comes to anyone, even those against me. These people are doing their jobs; if they are Americans, they are not my enemy."

"Nor ours," was Derek's reply. He then raised a hand in a reassuring gesture."Understood. Our primary goal is to protect you, but we'll do so within the boundaries you set. Jake will identify potential threats, and we'll handle them in the least confrontational way possible."

Already preparing for his mission, Jake adjusted the earpiece, connecting him to the rest of the team. "You have my word, Ryan. I'll be discreet and non-aggressive. But remember, if someone poses an immediate threat, I have to act swiftly and appropriately."

Ryan locked eyes with Jake, taking in this hulk of a man and recognizing the determination there. "Just promise me one thing: don't hurt anyone unless you're confident they're going to do serious damage to any of us on our team."

Jake gave a crisp nod, the picture of professionalism. "You have my word."

With that assurance, the team moved into action, each member settling into their respective roles. The room, which was filled with conversation and strategy just moments ago, now echoed with the silent efficiency of the Sentinel team.

Though still troubled by the swirling events around him, Ryan felt a glimmer of hope. With the formidable Sentinel Shield team at his side, he believed he stood a fighting chance against the secretive forces that seemed intent on ensnaring him.

A gentle knock at the door broke the heavy atmosphere that permeated the room. As the Sentinel operatives caught Ryan's brief nod, they retreated silently into their adjoining rooms. They discreetly closed the doors, with no lingering trace, like phantoms in the night, as if they had never been there.

Turning his attention to the entrance, Ryan checked the peephole and saw it was Dee. He opened the door to find her looking vulnerable yet determined. She hesitated for a moment, and Ryan motioned her in. As she crossed over, she leaned close to Ryan, her lips almost brushing his ear. She whispered so softly that the words were barely more than a breath, "We are being watched, and our conversations are probably monitored. I have to tell you something, and we need to be careful. We're both in trouble – deadly trouble. I had to see you. I needed you to know."

Outside in the hallway, Jake discreetly tailed the surveillance woman. From the corner of his eye, he noticed a shimmer of light reflecting off what seemed like a lens. He realized she was communicating with someone, likely giving a play-by-play of Dee's movements.

He followed her down a flight of stairs into a dimly lit passage.

As she rounded a corner, Jake took his chance, swiftly coming up behind her. Before she could utter a word, he'd silenced her with a hand and disarmed her with the other. Holding her firmly, he whispered, "Who sent you?"

She hesitated, her eyes darting around, searching for an escape route. But she quickly realized she was cornered.

Back in the room with Dee, Ryan was struggling to discern if she was lover or loather. The tension between them was formidable, like a pressure cooker on the verge of eruption. Memories of their shared past and the weight of present uncertainties hung in the air. But both tried to push it all aside, wanting to come to some understanding and move forward together.

Meanwhile, in the adjacent room, the Sentinel team leader, Derek, interrogated the Asian operative. Brandishing a Glock, his eyes bore into hers, searching for a hint of recognition or deceit. "Why are you following Harman? Who do you work for?"

The woman smirked, her demeanor icy cool. "I could ask you the same."

Derek leaned in, his voice dripping with authority. "That's not how this works, lady. Answer the question," as he waved his gun.

CHAPTER XXI

TRUTH UNVEILED

The silence in the room was deafening. Both Dee and Ryan were motionless for a moment. With its dimmed lights, the room seemed to hug the secrets they were about to share. Ryan stood, his back to Dee, gazing out the window at the hotel's expansive Japanese garden below, subtly lit and peaceful as a lake on a windless summer day. He stared at the stately former home of a nineteenth-century samurai who owned the property before it was converted into a hotel. *I feel like a daimyō, commanding four modern-day samurai of my very own.* Ryan thought and then turned to address Dee, "Go ahead, tell me why you betrayed me."

Dee took a deep breath, her eyes shimmering with tears, but her voice remained steady. "You must understand, my life wasn't my own from the start. My mother... She was beautiful, Ryan, a real beauty. But she was used, over and over, by those in power. They passed her around like she was a cheap bottle of vodka. I never knew my father until I was older, only that he was high-ranking within the GRU. He was the reason she was in that life, and he is the reason I am in it now. When my mother was no longer useful, they disposed of her. They will do the same to me."

Ryan, still not daring to trust her fully, glared silently.

She closed her eyes momentarily, collecting herself. "I was brought into the GRU's special training program as a child. They groomed me to be an asset, to seduce and gather intel. At first, I was proud. I thought I was serving my country, but it didn't take long to realize I was just a pawn, just like my mother."

A tear rolled down her cheek, but she brushed it away defiantly. "Sergei... my current handler, he sees me as his toy, his personal servant and whore. He would use me. He would remind me of my 'duties' to the motherland. Every time I resisted, he'd remind me of a man I had feelings for. It feels like a lifetime ago, but in my early years working for the GRU I was assigned to obtain missile secrets from a man who ran a German missile company. Real feelings developed, but my superiors would have none of that. My one moment of genuine affection... and they took it from me."

The memory twisted her face, "They made me watch as they suffocated him with a pillow. I watched him kick and struggle until he went limp. Then, they put him in a bathtub to make it look like he drowned in a hotel tub. They wanted to break me, to control me completely. They warned that the next time that I got too close to a mark, I would 'drown' too. I learned to shut down my feelings, to become numb. But then, you and I met..."

Her voice trailed off, and she looked into Ryan's eyes, vulnerability etched into every feature. "I didn't plan on this, on feeling this way about you. But I do. I think... I think I love you."

Ryan felt a crack in his armor, a very small crack. She had betrayed him. He was having difficulty getting over the feeling of being used and humiliated. Yet, a tiny seed of trust was planted. He had known deceit and betrayal but never at this level. She had proven she was an accomplished actor, yet the depth of Dee's pain seemed overwhelmingly authentic. He decided to take a baby step of trust,"The CIA is aware of all of this, Dee. If you stay with me, you're in danger, not just from the GRU but from them too."

A soft knock at the door interrupted their intense conversation. Ryan rose and opened the door. Derek Garner stepped in, followed by two members of his team. Their expressions were grim, revealing that they had overheard the confession. The atmosphere was tense.

Ryan looked around the room, shook his head, and said, "Gentleman, meet Dee. Dee, meet my protection team. Boys and Girls, new plan."

CHAPTER XXII

EVERYONE HAS A PLAN UNTIL THEY'RE PUNCHED IN THE MOUTH

Ryan gathered his team in the suite, where chairs, a couch, and a bed served as makeshift seating. He gestured for everyone to grab a drink and take a seat, his mind racing. The pieces on the chessboard were set. The first moves were made. He carefully mapped out how he proposed to outflank his opponents in the dangerous match they were now engaged in. With this team by his side, it was time to get this party started.

Before Ryan could outline his plan, Derek Garner stood and said, "In the rush of our initial activity, we didn't have time for formal introductions. Now that we have a moment, I want to introduce the team to both of you. I'm Derek Garner; I lead this team assigned to your protection."

He then pointed to each of his team members, "This is Phil Eichel; he's an expert defensive driver, and as you can see by looking at him, he can physically handle threats.

This is the inappropriately named Jake Little; besides his size, he's our backup driver and our electronics engineer. And finally, Richard "Don't-Call-Me-Dick" Kurtz," an expert marksman and black belt in three unique martial arts."

Each man nodded to Dee and Ryan as they were introduced. "What's the plan, Ryan? Where do we go from here?"

"Okay, Dee," Ryan began, his voice low but determined, "what's their plan for me? What are you supposed to do with me?"

Dee leaned forward and began to explain, "I'm to seduce you with promises of a life with me and money in exchange for your laptop with access to the latest version of Checkmate," Dee replied sheepishly with eyes pointed at the floor. "They want you and the software. They want you to help them implement the system."

Ryan raised an eyebrow, his mind already working on potential countermeasures. "Where does this take place?"

Dee looked up and met Ryan's eyes, knowing this was her chance to redeem her wrongs. She replied confidently, "Wherever I can lure you,"

Ryan's eyes narrowed as he considered their options. "Are your handlers aware that American intelligence agents are following me?"

Dee hesitated for a moment before responding, "I don't know. A surveillance team followed me in Budapest, and they didn't seem Russian. I was able to shake them. I let my handler know I was being followed and evaded surveillance. I don't think there is any reason they would believe it had anything to do with this assignment or that you were under surveillance."

"Dee, think hard on this one; think, in which nearby city do your people have the least amount of influence and control?

She thought for a minute and said, " Here, Hong Kong or Seoul… probably Hong Kong."

Ryan leaned back, deep in thought. Then he turned to Garner, who was silently observing the conversation. "Derek, can you get us a private jet, one that can carry the six of us and has the range to get us to Hanoi?"

Derek nodded, though he pointed out the potential financial implications. "I can, but that's outside my team's original assignment. I'll have to speak with my CEO to determine how that changes our financial arrangement."

Ryan considered the risks and rewards and decided to push the envelope. "Dee, how much are your people willing to pay for the laptop?"

"I don't know. To my knowledge, we've not paid for this kind of thing in the past."

Ryan continued his line of questioning, "Would they pay ten million, U.S.?"

Dee considered the figure for a moment. "I think they'd jump at that."

Ryan upped the ante, "How about twenty million?"

Dee hesitated before responding, "It's a stretch, but yes, I think they would."

Ryan had the plan forming in his mind and began to outline it.

"Okay, Derek, get me that plane and let me know how that changes our deal. I'll need us all to get on the plane with no one tailing us. File a flight plan to Hanoi; while in the air, we'll claim we have engine issues and request an emergency landing in Hong Kong. I want new identities for Dee and me. If you can do it, two or three sets each, delivered to us in Hong Kong if possible."

Dee stared at Ryan with admiration. She just saw another side of him that made him more desirable.

Derek whistled, realizing the complexity of the operation. He looked up at the ceiling and said, "This is probably going to significantly add to your bill, Ryan."

"Let me worry about that," Ryan scratched his chin and thought for a moment, "I don't want us in a hotel in Hong Kong; we'll need Sentinel to book us an Airbnb, something with a kitchen, enough bedrooms, and bathrooms for the six of us to be comfortable. We may be there for a while. It needs to be private and defensible."

Ryan felt he was forgetting something and then remembered a very important detail, "Okay, one more thing. We need to get out of here now. The CIA will be missing that lady in the other room. They must know we're on to them. We have to ditch the opposition's surveillance teams and catch our plane in secret."

"I'll get the company to book A rooms in a shell company name." Derek said, " How many rooms do we need, two for me and my team? Do I need three or four total?" He looked at Dee, who smiled at Ryan.

"Three rooms. Ryan replied, "No one should be alone during this phase."

Derek said, "All this is well outside our original scope. This is going to be expensive, Ryan."

Ryan's eyes were steely with determination as he responded, "That's okay, Derek. If I'm alive to receive your invoice, I'll have the money; otherwise, you can leave your bill in my coffin."

CHAPTER XXIII
TOKYO SUNRISE

Tokyo, Japan

The predawn haze of Tokyo painted the skyline in pastel hues of lilac and gold. As Richard Kurtz, the team's marksman, emerged from his room, the dimly lit corridor felt cramped and oppressive. The muted hum of the elevator and the occasional distant siren were the only signs of life in the otherwise silent hotel.

A subtle flicker of movement near the stairwell caught his eye. A man was loitering, his stance betraying unease, like a creature caught between fight and flight.

"You picked the wrong hallway," Kurtz whispered to himself. He swiftly pulled his Glock and aimed it at the man, his finger pressed to his lips, signaling the international sign language for shut-your-fucking-mouth. With a motion of his hand, he ushered the watcher into the room, where a bound Asian woman from the night before sat, her face a mask of fear. With practiced efficiency, Kurtz gagged and restrained the man with plastic zip ties.

"Seems you have company," Kurtz said to the woman, nodding at his new captive. With a final glance, he left them in the hands of his partner, Phil Eichel. A hulking figure, Phil's intimidating stature was belied by his gentle demeanor. Phil checked that the two agents were secured and prepared to leave.

Phil opened the door, adjusted his jacket, confirmed he was not being watched, and continued to the lobby, feeling the weight of Tokyo's early morning humidity. He quickly assessed the dimly lit garage and noticed the silver Toyota HiAce Cargo Van left for him by an unknown Tokyo-based Sentinel operative. Settling into the right-hand driver's seat, he waited by the hotel entrance, observing the passersby. "On station," Eichel murmured into his lapel.

The early morning sun cast long shadows across the hotel entrance, and almost immediately, the engine roar of a powerful car broke the quiet. The black Audi A8/S8 commanded the attention of the hotel's valets and secretive intelligence agency observers. Jake Little pulled the Audi to a halt in front of the hotel entrance. As the glass doors opened, Dee, Ryan, and Derek Garner – the latter with a barely concealed holstered pistol underneath his unzipped windbreaker – quickly boarded.

"No room for error," Derek reminded them, his eyes scanning the surrounding area.

Before the Audi left the gated driveway of the hotel, the ominous form of a black Infiniti QX60 with a driver and two passengers followed on their tail.

As per the plan, Eichel deftly blocked the exit with the van. Just as the CIA operatives from the Infiniti started to exit their vehicle, another black Audi, driven by Kurtz, sped to a stop, its tires screeching in protest. Eichel grinned and gave the CIA agents a mocking wave before taking the van keys, abandoning his van, and jumping into Kurtz's car. The pair sped away, leaving the frustrated CIA agents in their dust.

Fifty minutes later, the group found themselves aboard a sleek Dassault Falcon 2000LXS jet, the hum of engines and the soft plush seats offering a brief reprieve from the chaos.

Ryan, looking out of the window, whispered, "Sayonara Tokyo, nǐ hǎo, Hong Kong," marveling at the beauty even in their high-stakes escape.

"Hello, Sunrise," Derek remarked, looking down at the sun rising over the ocean to the east.

Ryan took a drink of orange juice and replied, almost to himself, "Let's hope it's not our last."

Somewhere Over The East China Sea

Inside the Dassault Falcon 2000LXS, the sterile smell of luxury leather and polished wood wafted throughout the cabin. The hum of the jet's engines acted as a reassuring lullaby in contrast to the adrenaline of the escape.

Ryan turned to Dee, his sharp, dark eyes searching her face for signs of distress. She had the calm and determined look of a veteran mercenary. He thought to himself, this kind of thing is standard operating procedure for her. He asked, "You good?"

Dee nodded, brushing a stray strand of hair behind her ear. "All good," she replied with a thumbs up.

Derek Garner, across from them, loosened his windbreaker, revealing his holstered SIG Sauer P220 pistol. "We made it out; that's what matters," he said, his tone carrying a hint of finality.

Phil Eichel, ever the gentle giant, passed around a tray of bottled water. "Stay hydrated. Stay frosty. We all need to be in top form for whatever comes next."

Suddenly, the jet jolted, spilling some water from the open bottles. The passengers exchanged worried glances. Eichel spoke into the internal phone system. "What's the situation, pilot?"

The reply was filled with static. "Air turbulence; expect some rough air ahead."

Dee, trying to steady herself, looked at Ryan. "Do you think they know where we are? The CIA, I mean."

Ryan frowned. "I don't think so. I trust these guys." motioning to Derek and his men. "They're pros, and we made a clean getaway back there."

Derek and his men were busy checking maps and instruments. Derek was speaking on his sat phone when he hung up; he looked at Ryan. "Minor plan changes. Our Hong Kong branch was unable to get a large, secure Airbnb."

Ryan looked on with concern as Derek continued.

"The changes will improve our safety," Derek continued. "Our company rented a home in Deep Water Bay; it's a near-perfect secluded location and easy to defend. Also, we had to add two local drivers to the team, so we don't have to screw around obtaining Hong Kong drivers' licenses which keeps us under the radar, and we will have the use of two of our powerful and heavy corporate BMW 7 Series vehicles. By adding two drivers to our team, we gain two additional operators with two more guns, and by avoiding rental cars, we're harder to trace. Unfortunately, your bill keeps adding up. The Boss says you're lucky you have a connection with Dex, or he'd be looking for a million-dollar deposit by now."

The flight attendant entered from the front cabin and said, "Folks, buckle up; we've started our final approach into Hong Kong."

Ryan thought to himself. I never liked the term "final approach." May this not be our final approach. May we have many more approaches in the future.

Langley, Virginia

Martha Kelly, CIA Counter Intelligence Section Chief, banged her fist on the table. Her face was red with fury. She sat across from Donald Folsom, the director of the two teams of field agents assigned to the Checkmate breach affair.

"You lost them?" she said, her voice trembling with rage. "You lost two of the most potentially dangerous people in our world?"

Folsom nodded, his face grim. "Yes, Director. They ghosted us."

"How could you lose them?" Kelly screamed. "You had two teams, twelve very experienced agents, people you told me we could count on. You told me your team would be like gum on a shoe. What happened, you run out of gum?"

"It was a well-coordinated escape," Folsom said. "It appears they had professional help."

"Russian agents?" Kelly asked.

Folsom shook his head. "We don't know. But they were good."

"Two of our agents were captured," Folsom continued. "They were tied up in a hotel room adjacent to Harman's. They report the captors spoke English like Americans."

Kelly closed her eyes for a moment, trying to calm her anger. "There's no traces of mobile phone activity, banking, or credit card transactions by either Volkova or Harman," she said. "They've vanished... what into thin air?"

Folsom nodded. "It's like they never existed."

"And we have eyes and ears on his wife, his Israeli friend, and that guy in London? "

"Yes, no signs of contact between Harman and any of them."

Kelly stood up and walked over to the window. She looked out at the crowded parking lot below, her mind racing. She needed to find Volkova and Harman; she thought of something. "I want a list of every private mercenary or protection agency that Harman might have hired. If Harman hired an American company for protection, how many could there be? We should have a list and contacts for them. Priority number one, get Harman and Volkova; number two, find who's helping them."

She turned away from the window and walked back to her desk. She sat down, picked up the phone, and asked her admin to get CIA Director Rogers on the phone. Two minutes later, her phone rang. She picked it up, "Director Rogers, we've lost them."

"This is a serious situation, Martha," the Director said. "I need you to do everything you can to find them."

"I will, sir," Kelly replied. "I promise."

She hung up the phone and took a deep breath. She was determined to succeed. She had to find Volkova and Harman. She had to find them before it was too late.

Kelly turned to Folsom. "We need to put all of our resources into finding them," she said. "Get on it now. I don't want to see you back here, Don, until you have them."

Folsom nodded. "I'm on it, Director."

Kelly watched as Folsom left the room. She knew that this was going to be a long night. But she was determined to find Volkova and Harman. She had to.

Blue Water Bay, Hong Kong

The BMWs made their way up the driveway of the property in Deep Water Bay, the wheels crunching against the gravel. The team exited the cars, taking in the spacious rented house with a mixture of appreciation and alertness.

The house wasn't a cozy little cottage. It was a mansion, a blend of modern architecture and traditional Chinese motifs. Tall glass windows gave a panoramic view of the South China Sea. Soft, ambient lights bathed the interiors, hinting at an understated luxury.

"We've got a bit of downtime," Derek said, taking the lead. "Let's pick our rooms and get settled."

Jake and the driver named Lin started off, taking the room closest to the main entrance – it made it easier for them to rotate in shifts. Phil and the other driver, Wong, took the second room, leaving the third for Derek and Kurtz. Dee and Ryan naturally gravitated towards the master bedroom with its king-sized bed and a view that looked out over the water.

The master suite was impressive, with a walk-in closet and a large bathroom featuring a rain shower and a soaking tub. Dee chuckled, "For a temporary setup, this isn't half bad."

Ryan and Dee checked out the spacious, well-appointed, high-tech kitchen set against the backdrop of a breathtaking view of the bay.

But perhaps the most enchanting feature of the kitchen was the open concept, which seamlessly connected it to a spacious outdoor terrace. Here, a luxurious al fresco dining area awaited, complete with a built-in barbecue and pizza oven, all set up for dining under the stars, with the gentle lapping of the bay waters in the background.

Ryan smirked, "If this is a safe house, I might get used to living on the run."

The pool, its water gleaming under the soft lights, caught everyone's attention. "No time for a swim now," Dee said, "but later, who knows?"

Next, they found a well-equipped gym. There was a sauna adjacent to the gym and a steam room just a few steps away from the sauna.

After everyone unpacked, Derek assigned Wong and Phil grocery duty. "We'll need supplies if we're holing up here for a while," He commented.

Lin and Jake, meanwhile, began their patrol, walking the perimeter of the house, setting up discreet security cameras, motion sensors, and checking for vulnerabilities.

Inside the well-appointed, spacious living room, Derek powered up his laptop and connected it to a projector. Dee, Ryan, and the rest gathered around, maps and plans spread out on the coffee table.

Ryan took control, "Alright, so Dee," he began, "You're going to make the call to Sergei."

Dee nodded, taking a deep breath. "Yes, I'll set up the meet. I'll tell him Ryan has agreed to work with us, but he requires twenty million U.S. dollars."

Ryan rubbed his temples, the weight of the situation pressing on him. "We have to make this work," he murmured under his breath, then said to Derek, "I'm going to need you to set up two numbered accounts for me in the Caymans."

He stopped for a minute, thinking, and then continued, "I'll go to the meet with Sergei sans the laptop; I'll keep that somewhere close. It's my only leverage. As soon as they get their hands on the PC, the balance of power shifts from us to them. Derek, once your people confirm the money is in the first account, I'll take Sergei to the laptop. Then I want your people to take your cut and transfer the rest to my second account. I don't want these goons to know where the money ended up."

Dee chimed in, "I'm going with you."

Ryan didn't fully trust her and thought he'd have better odds on his own, "No, Dee, that's not happening; we don't need both of us at risk," he replied.

Dee nodded, crossed her arms, and said, "I don't like it."

"Neither do I," replied Ryan, "But we'll all like it when it's over."

Derek said, "We'll have our team nearby, on foot and in vehicles. Ryan, we will sew a tracker and mic into your clothes. We'll be able to hear everything that's said and track your every movement."

The room settled into a focused silence, with each team member mentally preparing for the events to come. Outside, the sun began to set over Deep Water Bay, casting an orange-red glow on the calm waters. It was a peaceful scene, a stark contrast to the storm that was brewing for the team.

Dee picked up the phone and called Sergei; the conversation was in Russian. When she disconnected, she reported, "He will need to discuss your terms and the money with his bosses. He thinks he can get what you ask. He said he could be in Hong Kong by Tuesday. He'll call us sometime after that and give us the meeting place one hour prior. He insists that I come with you."

"I don't like that, but we'll see," Ryan replied.

Derek shook his head in admiration, "One hour to prep. That's good tradecraft. It won't give us much time to set up surveillance. But, we'll be ready."

Derek motioned to Richard Kurtz to join him in Derek's bedroom. "Okay, Kurtz, did you understand the conversation?"

"I understood everything she said, he replied."

"...And?"

"It sounded legit, Captain. But I only heard her side of the conversation. What I heard doesn't matter much. She may be cautious thinking one of us knows Russian."

"True." Derek replied, "I don't know if we can trust her. Stay close." The two men returned to the living room.

Ryan said, "That gives us a minimum of two days to rest, plan, and think about what we have missed."

As Derek and Kurtz left the room, Ryan stood looking out at the bay, lit by the orange sun setting over the hills across the bay by the Repulse Bay Road. Without a word, he turned and walked to the master bedroom. He lay down on the bed, staring while his mind was lost in thought. Unaware of his surroundings, his thoughts meandered to Phoebe, his radiant, young daughter with her bubbly laughter and a penchant for asking a thousand questions. He was coming to the realization that he may never see her again, which caused a sharp ache in his chest. Would she be safe? Would she understand why her father had suddenly disappeared from her life?

He thought to himself, "If I have to stay away from her to keep her safe, I will. Whatever happens to me… if I make it out of this damn mess, I need to figure out a way to keep my little girl safe, secure, and well cared for."

Dee slid the balcony door open, the scent of saltwater filling the room, interrupting his morose mental self-flagellation. "Am I interrupting? You okay?" she whispered, sat next to him, and thought to herself, will he ever forgive and trust me?

Ryan turned to look at her. "I was thinking about Phoebe. I'm dragging her into this mess. I can't bear the thought of never seeing her again."

"You mean, I dragged you into this mess," she replied, "And I will never be able to make that up to you, Ryan."

Taking in her words, he chewed on them without responding. Dee lay down next to him on the bed, both of them just lying there, quietly staring up at the ceiling.

CHAPTER XXIV

TELL ME NO SECRETS

In Bedford, Massachusetts, Roger Scranton, CEO of Sentinel Shield, sat behind a desk in his spacious corner office, located in a two-story red brick building just off Route 128. As Scranton reviewed routine paperwork, his admin knocked and showed Ned Ransom into the room.

Ransom, a CIA agent, called earlier in the morning and demanded a meeting before the end of the day. Scranton intentionally pointed the CIA man to the "torture" chair. A seat he reserved for unwanted visitors. The seat cushions of Ransom's uncomfortable chair had lost its plumpness, leaving behind a sagging, lumpy surface that offered no support to its unfortunate occupant. Sitting on it, he felt like he was sinking into a black hole of discomfort, as if the chair was actively conspiring against him for daring to plop his ass upon it.

Scranton's office was decorated with framed commendations, a framed pair of crossed swords, his service medals, and a dozen or so photos of Roger and fellow soldiers with whom he served throughout his military career. Behind his head, and thankfully unnoticed by Ransom, was a picture of two smiling special operators standing close together in battle fatigues, both holding helmets and M4A1 Carbine rifles in their hands. One of the soldiers was Scranton. The other was aiCheckmate's Dex Johnson.

"I'm sorry, I can't help you, Mr. Ransom. I don't know anything about these people you lost."

"That's too bad, Mr. Scranton," Ransom replied, "I'd hate to find out you were holding back on us. There would be consequences, and you'd be sorry if we found you were aiding or harboring a national security threat."

"Listen, Ransom, I don't take kindly to threats. I don't know anything about your problems, and I don't give a rat's ass if you find those people or not. What I do know is that had you hired my firm to watch them in the first place, they never would have gone missing. We'd know exactly where they were right now. You see, we don't suck at our jobs."

Unable to tamp down his anger, Ransom replied, "You're making enemies of the wrong people, Scranton."

"Hell, even if I did know where these people were, I wouldn't tell you. My stock and trade is very similar to yours. It relies on my complete discretion. I can't talk about my missions, the same as you can't tell me about yours."

Roger continued ranting on his figurative soap box, "Mr. Ransom, in America, we have laws, and let me tell you about them. This here where we're sitting is the good old U.S. of A., and you are the not-so-good old C.I. of A., which means you have no authority here, so if you want to threaten me, you better come back with someone from the good old F.B. of I. or anyone with the proper initials and authorization to operate in this here great country and oh, make sure they bring a warrant. Savvy?"

"Thank you, Mr. Scranton. You've made it clear whose side you're on. You'll hear from us again."

"I look forward to it... Oh, and one more thing," Scranton added. "Before you go, I'll offer this one-time deal. You tell me who killed Kennedy, and I'll open up my file room for you. Otherwise, come back with a warrant. Now, seeing as you can't keep track of two civilians, can I trust you to find yourself out?" Scranton grinned. Ned, red-faced and without a grin, walked out the door and turned left, then realized his mistake and turned to his right to leave.

Watching him, Scranton's grin grew wider as he stifled a chuckle.

CHAPTER XXV

DOMESTIC COMFORT

Ryan cleared his head, got up from the bed, and said, "Let's take advantage of the hot tub."

They donned bathing suits from their packed clothing and walked through the living room to discover the domestic scene of Wong's cooking. Exotic aromas filled the room as Wong was chopping vegetables, boiling liquids, and sizzling meats on the stove. Wong was to be tonight's chef. Derek was staring at his computer, ensuring that all the intricate details of the next few days were in place.

Jake walked in from his bedroom and said he was doing laundry. He asked if Ryan and Dee had clothes that needed washing. Lin and Richard were patrolling the grounds. Phil was in the gym working out.

Ryan and Dee eased into the hot tub, the warm bubbles surrounding them like a cocoon. The night was clear, stars glittering overhead, the scene's serenity juxtaposed with the chaos of their lives. Ryan looked at Dee and said, "We're committed; there's no turning back now."

Derek, having heard snippets of their conversation, joined them. "The thing about our line of work," he began with a sigh, "is that there's rarely a way back. We cross lines that can't be uncrossed."

Ryan grimaced and replied, "Our line of work… three weeks ago, I wasn't in our line of work."

Dee gazed at the water, ripples reflecting the ambient light. "The CIA and the GRU will hunt us down forever. Every international agency will have our faces on their screens."

"We'll figure out how to deal with that, Dee; we are both going to be on the Most Wanted list of many countries." Ryan leaned back, letting the water lap against his neck, and marveled at the night sky.

Later, Ryan grabbed Derek for a private moment. "What's happening with our new identity papers?"

Derek replied. "They're in the works. That's what I was checking on the computer. They should be ready in three more days. I just need to figure out how to get them from Singapore to wherever we are when we need them."

Ryan, looking dead serious, said, "Derek, I would like all our pursuers to think I'm dead after I trade the laptop. I don't want the Russians, or anyone for that matter, to use my daughter to get to me. I need them to believe there is no me. Everyone, friend and foe must believe I am dead."

"You understand what you're saying, Ryan?" Derek looked at Ryan in disbelief, and he added. "You're cutting all ties with her. You'll likely never see her again."

Ryan's voice cracked, and his eyes turned glassy; he said, "I've gone over this in my mind, and as much as this pains me, I know that killing Ryan Harman is the only way of keeping Phoebe Harman alive and safe. So yes, Ryan Harman must die."

Wong broke the tension as he announced, "Dinner's ready!"

As Jake and Phil took their shift patrolling the grounds, the rest of the team gathered around the dining table to enjoy Wong's excellent Cantonese dinner. The fragrant aromas that had filled the room now emanated from the dishes placed before them.

Wong had outdone himself, preparing a feast showcasing Cantonese cuisine's rich flavors. Plates of succulent sweet and sour pork, glazed with a perfect balance of tangy and sweet sauce, were surrounded by bowls of fluffy white rice. Platters of delicate dim sum and stir-fried vegetables glistened with a glossy sheen, the vibrant colors a testament to their freshness.

Delectable aromas wafted through the air as the team dug into the dishes. The sweet and savory notes of the cuisine danced on their taste buds, a momentary escape from the high-stress mission on which they were about to embark.

There was food, beer, wine, and laughter. Amid the clinking of glasses, the team engaged in convivial conversation. They discussed past missions, shared humorous anecdotes, and found solace in the camaraderie acquired when a group of people who share a common goal find themselves under intense pressure. Beneath the warm glow of good food, good company, and camaraderie, there was an undertone of tension. In the back of everyone's mind, how many of us may be having our last meal?

CHAPTER XXVI

PLANS AND PEACE

The following day, with the light filtering through the drapes of the master suite Dee and Ryan awoke entangled in each other's bodies. Ryan had come to terms with a host of issues, his impending divorce and his forced estrangement from Phoebe. Dee stirred, and he felt her warm breath against his chest. He was about to enter a new life as a new man with a new name.

His feelings about Dee were still unclear; he didn't blame her for her circumstances... shit happens, and the shit that happened to her shouldn't happen to anyone. He was absolutely taken by her physical beauty, her smarts, and he enjoyed her company. But he didn't know if he completely trusted her. And he wondered if the excitement and danger she represented was a factor in his attraction to her. He believed he might be in love with her in a way that he had never felt for Amy. But can you love someone you don't fully trust?

He stealthily left the bed without waking Dee and went to the bathroom. The warm cascade of water enveloped him as he stepped into the shower, the steam weaving tendrils around him, encasing him in solitude. Within this misty sanctuary, he always felt clarity, as if each droplet held the power to wash away distractions and uncertainty. He did some of his best thinking in the shower. Thoughts swirled around him, mingling with the steam, taking form and structure as the water rhythmically pelted his skin.

He dried off with extra-large, thick, soft towels hanging on a towel heater near the shower. Feeling invigorated and clear-headed, he was ready... but ready for what? Ready to wait for the call. He didn't want to think further than that; his mantra had always been, first thing first, second thing, never.

Conventional wisdom equated superior strategic planning to

master-level chess, where one consistently thinks several moves in advance. Ryan believed that kind of detailed planning was wasted energy. He practiced what he called just-in-time strategic planning. Planning requires having an end goal and a set of operating principles, taking inventory of your assets and liabilities, and then instead of worrying about the three ifs and a maybe you might encounter down the road, one should concentrate on the next if. This morning, he was planning for the next if, the issues right in front of him, weighed the probabilities, and changed his plan to account for the next if.

Dressed in shorts and a T-shirt, he walked into the living room, more of a great-room combination of living room/dining room, connected to the open kitchen. Dee was awake and now sitting back on the couch, her tan legs outstretched with her bare feet resting on a mahogany coffee table. She was watching the BBC, holding a half-full mug of black coffee.

Derek and Jake were in the other half of the room, what the team had begun referring to as the war room. The war room was a dining area off the kitchen; the two men were seated on two bamboo and wicker chairs around a large brass and smoked glass dining room table.

Ryan took a moment, letting the gravity of the situation settle, then approached the table with an assertive stride. He raised his hand in a beckoning gesture, signaling Dee to join them. The atmosphere was thick with anticipation, each face looking up at him expectantly.

With a half smile that held more gravity than jest, he began, "Here's the deal," Ryan explained. "I changed my mind, Dee. We can go to the meet together. We will take one of the BMWs." Ryan continued with a broad brush outline of a long and detailed plan. When he was finished, he looked at Dee, "OK?"

"This has been your show-up until now, and so far, it's worked. This variation of the plan adds risk, but it could work. Trust me, Ryan, I will do my part."

Ryan looked at Derek, "And you?"

Derek nodded, his expression pensive. "Your idea is as solid as any I could come up with," he conceded. He paused for a moment, rubbing his chin thoughtfully. "We'll acquire the required equipment. A few of the items we'll need are not in our standard kit. Both you and Dee will be wired with trackers and mics. I'll station two of our guys in another car nearby while the others will be strategically positioned in the neighborhood on foot. As for me, I'll be back here, overseeing everything via the comms and monitoring your locations." He sighed deeply, a mix of apprehension and hope in his eyes. "This is a crazy plan, but I've come out of crazier plans with worse odds without a scratch."

Upon the meeting's completion, Derek pulled Ryan aside, "Got a minute?"

"Sure," and the two walked into Derek's bedroom. Derek closed the door and, in a hushed tone, said, "You're putting your life in her hands. Are you a hundred percent sure you can trust her?"

Ryan scratched his head and looked at the closed door, "Derek, I don't trust anyone, even me, one hundred percent. On a scale of one to ten, where Sergei is a one, and I'm a nine, I'd rate her a seven," paused a few seconds, raised his eyebrows, and continued," maybe a six."

Derek looked concerned and asked, "Where am I on that scale?"

Ryan smiled, hand on his shoulder, and replied, "I trust you more than I trust myself, Captain. But nobody gets a ten."

As they left the room, Dee looked at Ryan, a look of concern on her face, "Up for hanging at the pool?" Ryan nodded his assent, and they walked into their room to change. Ryan closed the door, Dee stepped close, and looked up at his eyes, "What was that about?"

"What do you mean, with Derek?" He took a slight step back and put his hand affectionately on her chin; in an attempt to allay any of her fears, he said, "Derek has some personal issues, and he wanted me to know that it wouldn't affect his performance." Dee started to pull on her swimsuit, and once again, he thought, I wish I had a better poker face.

While Derek dispatched Lin and Phil to gather the necessary equipment to bring their plan to life, Wong and Jake started their patrol shift around the premises. Seeking a brief reprieve from the tension, Ryan and Dee found themselves by the pool. Ryan's eyes darted to the speaker system; the idea of soft melodies filling the air appealed to him. Yet, having abandoned his phone to elude CIA detection, he was without his usual playlist.

Approaching the team inside, he inquired, "Anyone here have Spotify? I'd like to pipe it through the house's sound system?" Jake, ever eager to assist, volunteered. "How about some Marc Cohn?" Ryan suggested. The first notes of a familiar tune began to drift out, and the duo settled into plush lounge chairs, their fingers entwined. The afternoon sun warmed their skin, tempered by a gentle seventy-eight-degree autumn breeze.

Dee decided to take a dip. Ryan watched as she glided through the water, her strokes powerful yet graceful, causing barely a ripple on the surface. Marc Cohn's excellent cover of Paul McCartney's, Maybe I'm Amazed, played softly in the background. A pang of longing and sadness struck him. Life with Dee might promise many beautiful days like this, but the void left by his estranged daughter—a constant, glowing presence in his life—loomed large in his heart.

Ryan fell asleep on the lounge chair, listening to Cohn's tribute to the house the great painter Frederic Church built on the Hudson River, Olana. For a short moment, everything was good.

At eight-eleven p.m., Dee's phone rang. The team surrounded her as she took the call in the living room; they were all gathered there, having after-dinner beers and reminiscing about past lives, loves, missions, and lost friends. Dee looked at the caller ID and nodded her head at Ryan. She answered in Russian, "PREE-vyet?" Ryan tried to read Dee's face as Kurtz moved closer in order to hear as much of the conversation on the other side as possible. When she hung up, she coolly announced, "They're in. It's a go."

CHAPTER XXVII
TRANSFER OF POWER

Just before nine p.m., Ryan and Dee exited their safe house and stepped out into the breezy and quiet Deep Water Bay evening. They approached their garage, where Ryan took position behind the right-hand driver's seat of the BMW. The leather felt cool beneath his fingers as he adjusted the settings, thankful it was an automatic; he could never use his left hand to work a stick-shift.

After the pleasant afternoon, a north wind blew in a humid chill on this late Hong Kong October evening, its fingers slipping through the densely built neighborhoods.

Dee settled next to him. She shot a glance to the backseat, her face a mixture of concern and curiosity. "Where's the laptop?"

"I've got that covered," Ryan said cryptically, his eyes focused ahead. He missed Dee's fleeting look of confusion, her gaze drawn to him, as he tucked a nine-inch bolster stiletto knife into his black windbreaker pocket. As he remotely activated the garage door, the engine's rumble echoed throughout, a cacophony of sounds signifying raw power.

Derek was left to oversee operations from the base, surrounded by an array of screens in their makeshift war room. Thirty minutes prior, the other five members of the team left in Lin's car. When they were in the vicinity of the meeting, Wong, Jake, and Eichel exited the car and took up positions, blending in with the locals, their seemingly casual strolls concealing their alertness. Kurtz and Lin took their places, a block away from the meeting location in the vehicle, eyes peeled and ears tuned to the comms traffic.

Navigating through the Sai Ying Pun neighborhood, Dee and Ryan absorbed the faint aroma of frying fish spices and the distinctive scent of Hong Kong's streets wafting through the car's vents. They passed the illuminated sign of the meeting location, Tsui Wah restaurant. The restaurant windows fogged up with the warmth and hustle of diners within. A short distance away, Ryan eased the BMW into an alley, the dim overhead lights casting elongated shadows on the cobblestones. The two made their way to the restaurant, its door emitting a brief jingle as they stepped inside.

The soft chatter of the few patrons filled the air, accompanied by the clinking of dishes and chopsticks. At the back, Sergei was an unmistakable slovenly presence, noodles dripping from his chopsticks, the trail lost within the thickets of his unkempt beard. His eyes, however, were sharp and met Dee's immediately, giving a nod of acknowledgment.

Ryan, trailing behind Dee, couldn't help but scrutinize Sergei's appearance. The man's bulky frame was squeezed into an ill-fitting brown suit that had seen better days. They took their seats, Sergei's tea-stained teeth flecked with remnants of his meal, bared in a grin. "So nice to meet you, Mr. Harman; I've heard many things about you," he said, leaving the air thick with unspoken implications.

Suppressing the emotions threatening to boil over, Ryan replied evenly, "Yes, Dee has told me about you, too. Let's get this over with."

"What's your hurry, Mr. Harman? Don't be that way." The Russian belched, then wiped spittle, soup, and noodles from his beard before continuing, "We're about to join together in a prosperous partnership. Sit, let us break bread together. You and I are going to join in a lasting relationship and become good friends."

"No fucking way. Once the transfers are made, I'm done with this shit and with you," Ryan said, glaring at the dangerous slob across the table.

"Not so quick, Mr. Harman. We will need you to work with us to help make sure we implement Checkmate correctly and to advise us until we are proficient in the software. So the laptop and you will be coming with me."

Once again, Ryan's attempt at a poker face failed him, revealing a clear trace of hatred.

Caught between them, Dee felt the tension hanging in the air like the humidity outside. "What now, Sergei? Let's get this moving."

Sergei, enjoying his display of power, toyed with the idea of prolonging the encounter, like a cat torturing before devouring a cornered rat. "I thought we'd share a meal together first, but if you're eager, then alright. Dee, I was told Ryan would bring his laptop. I don't see a laptop."

Ryan leaned in slightly, a calculated move. "You'll get the laptop once I get a call from my banker confirming the transfer." As he spoke, he slid a clamshell burner phone onto the table.

Sergei chuckled, clearly impressed. "A smart man, nice thinking, Mr. Harman," then nodded at Dee, "Are you armed, as I asked?"

"Da, of course." Her response was curt, almost mechanical.

Sergei's eyes flitted between the two, savoring his control over the situation. "Mr. Harman, as you may know, Dee works for me. You should thank me; I am the one who ordered her to sleep with you. She's good… no?"

This comment, designed to enrage Ryan, hit its mark. Ryan bared his teeth, focused on the end game, calmed himself, and replied, "Can we move this along."

"I'll arrange the money transfer as you requested. But if there's no laptop, or any attempt at deceit," Segie paused for dramatic effect, "Dee will not sleep with you again. Instead, she will use her pistol to put you down for your final sleep. If I don't get the laptop, you won't get to spend that money. You understand the dead don't get to spend money; is that clear?"

Ryan's gaze shifted to Dee, who silently affirmed the threat with a subtle display of her Beretta. He swallowed hard, the weight of the situation sinking in. "You would do that?"

"Ryan, you're not a bad guy, but this is my job and my country. This is business, nothing personal."

"You will betray me for this pig?" Ryan said, nodding his head towards Sergei.

"I work for my country, not him, not you, not any man," she replied.

At that, Sergei giggled like a little boy. "Pig, you say? Is that any way to talk to your new partner?" He then tapped a few commands into his iPhone and smirked. "It is done; the money has been transferred."

Moments later, the shrill ring of Ryan's phone sliced through the thick atmosphere. After a brief exchange, he placed the phone down, addressing the Russians. "It's confirmed. Follow me, and I will get the laptop for you."

Sergei paid the bill before he and Dee followed Ryan, who retraced his steps back to the alley and the car. Ryan stepped to the back of the vehicle, opened the trunk, and lifted the spare tire cover, revealing the laptop. Sergei leaned in and grabbed the laptop to inspect it. Ryan reached for his stiletto, and Dee called out, "Watch out, Serj, he has a knife." The loud crack of a sudden gunshot broke the quiet of the Hong Kong night. The echo reverberated off the close walls, and Ryan's body hit the ground, blood slowly painting the cobblestones, his fingers just shy of the open knife.

Dee, her face impassive, put a hand on his neck and felt his carotid artery, confirming Ryan was no longer amongst the living. "No pulse," she announced and removed Harman's knife from the scene.

Sergei's voice trembled, a mix of disappointment, delight, and adrenaline evident in his tone. "I have the laptop, and thanks to you, Deandra, I have my life. Harman was a bonus. Now, time's against us. We need to get away from here quickly!"

They rushed from the alley to the main thoroughfare as the night swallowed their presence. The only evidence of their encounter was a lifeless body lying in the shadows and a lingering echo. Sergei hailed a taxi. Less than ninety seconds after the shot rang out in the alley, Dee and Sergei were rushing to safety with the laptop under his arm.

In a dark Sai Ying Pun alley, a dimly lit street lamp casts its yellow light on a giant gray rat, edging towards a lifeless body lying in a pool of blood.

Part III - Checkmate

"Life is a game that must be played, but in the end, it's checkmate that counts."

– Mark Twain

CHAPTER XXVIII
DEE'S GIFT

Kowloon, Hong Kong

The wind transformed into a warm breeze. The humid evening air hung heavily over Tai Kok Tsui Road in Kowloon. As street lights cast a soft, diffused glow, they illuminated the Dorsett Mongkok Hotel's sleek glass facade.

A red Toyota Crown Comfort urban taxi pulled up to the hotel entrance, its brakes letting out a soft squeak. From its dim interior emerged two incongruous figures: a disheveled, corpulent man in his fifties and a captivating, dark-haired beauty. Without exchanging a word, Dee trailed behind Sergei, their faces revealing none of the evening's drama; they stepped quickly, their footsteps echoing slightly in the hushed ambiance as they made their way to Sergei's room on the third-floor room.

Once inside, Sergei promptly dialed a number. "We will be connected in fifteen minutes," he said with an air of authority. He placed the PC on the polished wooden desk, turned it on, and hesitated momentarily when confronted with the prompt, "Enter Your PIN Code."

"Do you know his code, Dee?" he inquired, an edge of impatience in his voice.

Sliding gracefully into the desk chair behind the keyboard, Dee entered Ryan's pin code with a practiced hand. "Of course, Sergei," she responded with a smirk. "I'm not some silly trollop who just walked in off the street; I'll remind you I'm a well-trained professional. I know Ryan's passcodes, his social security number, what he had for breakfast on his eighteenth birthday, his mother's birthday... everything."

Sergei connected the laptop to the hotel's WiFi, initiated the VPN, and logged into the Internet Research Agency in St. Petersburg, handing the baton to Dimitri and Alexi in St. Petersburg.

St. Petersburg, Russia

Meanwhile, thousands of miles away in St. Petersburg, Dimitri's eyes gleamed with anticipation. Watching the progress bar on his screen, he leaned over to his partner Alexi and announced, "Athena came through for us. Checkmate Version 1b, the commercial release, is downloading now." They exchanged triumphant grins, eagerly anticipating the accolades and rewards their triumph would bring.

Computers hummed, characters kept streaming across the screens, and the two men watched the progress with anticipation as they envisioned the medals, rubles, and women they would soon be swimming in after the evening's success.

Kowloon, Hong Kong

Back in the dimly lit room in Kowloon, Sergei, emboldened by his victory, poured himself and Dee miniature bottles of vodka from the minibar. He unbuttoned his shirt, revealing his hairy chest covering his sagging breasts and rotund belly. As he approached her, his intentions clear, he leered at her and said, "Now Zaychik," Russian for little bunny, "with Harman dispatched, I no longer have to share you. Now you are all mine."

Dee smiled, looking forward to embracing this man who had exerted so much control over her life. She hugged him as she deftly reached into her purse, producing Ryan's fallen stiletto. Without a moment's hesitation, she drove the blade deep into Sergei's abdomen. She chose the knife, believing a quick death was too kind for this man.

He collapsed to his knees, gasping in agony, taking satisfaction from his pain and the recognition of betrayal, she coldly declared, "No, durak, " Russian for fool, "now, you are mine." Dee met his gaze with an icy stare and added, "I am no longer your whore. I am no longer Russia's tool." She stared into his eyes, savoring her controller's recognition that she was now the one in control.

As the life drained from his eyes and blood oozed from his mouth and wounds, Dee grabbed a nearby pillow, pressed it against his face, buried her Beretta deep within the cushioned barrier to dampen the noise. When she felt the barrel push against his forehead, she murmured, "This is for Victor and for Ryan."

Contrary to what Dee had seen in films, there was a loud crack. Her shot was only slightly muffled by the pillow. Dee quickly exited the room, leaving Sergei's lifeless corpse behind.

Sai Ying Pun, Hong Kong

Amidst the maze of narrow streets and alleyways Ryan's body lay there, lifeless and alone. When enough time had passed, and he was certain his would-be murderers were gone, he lifted his head. With a soft grunt, he pushed himself up and whispered, "All clear." The words meant for his team were relayed through the concealed transmitter. He quickly shed his shirt, discarding the now-useless blood-squib pack that had been secured to his chest. Within a few minutes, Kurtz and Lin arrived in their car. Kurtz left the vehicle and held the door for Ryan, urging, "Get in; let's get you out of here. The others are on their way. I'll wait here with your car, and we will join you at the safe house."

As Lin drove carefully, not too fast or too slow, avoiding any unwanted attention from the authorities, they made their way towards the safe house. Derek's voice crackled over the comms, "Dee's in Kowloon. From the chatter I'm picking up, it seems all is going according to plan."

Ryan quickly responded, "Let us know when she's done, Derek."

"Of course."

Deep Water Bay, Hong Kong

The ride to the safe house was smooth, the cityscape blurring past. The atmosphere in the car was thick with tension. Fifteen minutes after the first car arrived safely at the Deep Water Bay refuge, the second car arrived with the rest of the team, minus Dee. They huddled around Derek, anxiously listening to Dee's transmitter. They heard a scuffle and a grunt from Sergei, a gunshot, and moments later, Dee's voice, filled with a mix of exhaustion and exhilaration, came through on the speaker. "It's done. I'm on my way."

CHAPTER XXIX

RIPPLES OF FATE

Deep Water Bay, Hong Kong

The moonlight shimmered over the tranquil waters of Deep Water Bay, casting an ethereal glow over the sheltered cove. The anxiety of pursuit by the CIA had faded, and the menace of Sergei had been eliminated. Though momentarily at ease, every member of this newly formed tribe of kindred spirits knew that the water temperature had cooled by a degree or two. But the water was still hot, and the heat was still on.

To emphasize the continued danger, Derek remarked, "We may have taken the lead in this inning. But to quote Yogi Berra, It ain't over till it's over."

A breeze carried the scent of saltwater as the team went into a more relaxed mode, shifting to one-man patrol rotations. Ryan, seeking to bring a touch of normalcy, proposed he would be tonight's chef. He scribbled down a shopping list, handing it over to Wong and Jake, who were eager for a mundane task amidst the mayhem. Jake looked at the list and said to no one in particular, "Nice, steak night. I like that."

"It's the only thing I know how to cook," replied Ryan.

Inside their quarters, Ryan and Dee lounged on their bed. In his mind, Ryan reviewed the past two weeks. Though he never revealed it to Dee, he thought his chances of succeeding and surviving were less than fifty percent at best. There were too many moving pieces, too many unknowns. The plan required precise timing, flawless execution, and luck... mostly luck, lots of luck. Luck is a fickle mistress, as unpredictable as she is unreliable. Yet, now they were here, almost safe, almost done.

Ryan looked at Dee and said, "For a moment there, I was worried; what if you mixed up the blank with the live rounds when you loaded your clip?"

"Hey, cowboy, you should've focused more on your part in our theatrical performance. You were lucky Sergei was looking the other way during your Razzie-worthy, dramatic death scene. That was the worst, most amateurish acting performance I've ever witnessed," she scolded, shaking her head in mock disappointment. "I can hardly believe we spent all that time rehearsing your death only to watch you nearly bungle it. If we were on a Broadway stage instead of a Hong Kong back alley, your exaggerated, comedic tumble would have had the audience roaring with laughter. You were channeling Charlie Chaplin when you should have channeled Sir Lawrence Olivier."

The couple settled down in the dim, tranquil light that created a haven for them to share whispered dreams and fears about a future neither was certain of. Ryan was excited about the prospect of spending the rest of his life with this exciting, capable woman, yet in the back of his mind and in his heart, that ache kept coming back. Ryan would never see Phoebe again.

St. Petersburg, Russia

A sense of urgency cloaked the air as Dimitri and Alexi were ushered into the opulent office of the Internet Research Agency's commanding officer. The room, lavishly adorned and illuminated by a grand chandelier, was a stark contrast to the bleak St. Petersburg weather outside.

Smoking a cigar, sporting a radiant glow in his eyes, and the irrepressible smile of an expecting father, the General beckoned them closer from behind his mahogany desk. "Sit, Gentlemen, pour yourselves some vodka. Now, update me on our progress."

Swirling his glass, Alexi replied, "Everything appears to be on track. We anticipate a very favorable outcome in the next few hours."

The General's eyes sparkled, "Excellent. Your success will not go unrewarded."

Moscow, Russia

At the GRU headquarters, the atmosphere was thick with anxiety. Sergei's absence had sent ripples of unease through the ranks. He missed his last three scheduled check-ins. When called, his phone rang over to voicemail, and his unresponsiveness set alarms ringing. On reaching out to the Internet Research Agency, they were comforted to know that the software was in place. Yet, Colonel Ivanov was growing impatient for details on Sergei, Harman, and Athena's whereabouts.

Burlingame, Northern California

The humming servers of aiCheckmate were interrupted by urgent whispers. The InfoSec team detected an anomaly—data packets originating from Ryan Harman's laptop and confirmed by his digital signature made contact with the aiCheckmate servers. As the data flow intensified, alarms sounded. One of the operators dialed Bernard Milford, the company's Chief Information Officer, who looked at his computer, read the packets passing through cyberspace, pressed a few keys, and scrutinized the transmission. Realizing the potential ramifications, he instinctively reached for his phone, dialing Seb's number.

Virginia Waters, United Kingdom - Herzliya, Israel

Raj had settled down to watch a grudge match rivalry game between his beloved Celtic FC and their hated rivals, the Rangers. This picturesque afternoon in Virginia Waters was disturbed by the shrill ringing of Raj's phone. The caller ID flashed "Avi." Anticipating a casual catch-up, he answered cheerfully, "Hi Avi, why would you be disturbing me on my footie night? You're taking me away from me Celtics."

Avi replied in a choked tone, "Raj, I am not calling with good news."

Not sensing Avi's despair, Raj joked, "You're not quitting me now, are you lad?"

"There's no other way to tell you this, Raj; I'm just going to say it. Ryan is dead."

"Dead? "Raj gasped and dropped to the floor, his beer tanker spilling. He was struggling to find the words. Hearing his fall, his wife Nina entered the room, saw the distress in her husband's face, and put her hand to her mouth as she moved to hold him; she whispered, "What?"

Raj put the phone on speaker, "Avi... how?"

"My Mossad contacts tell me the Russians shot him in Hong Kong. And then disposed of the body. I have to go; you were my first call. Now I have to find a way to break this to Amy."

Raj composed himself and said, "I have no words, Avi. Okay, you call Amy. I will call Seb and break it to him."

St Petersburg, Russia

Alexi and Dimitri closely watched their progress, anticipating a triumphant mission report, now tasting the glory and making celebration plans in their minds, when suddenly, all the screens in the room went dark. "Not again," Alexi said to himself. They both grappled with the systems, desperately trying to restore them, but their efforts proved futile. After two hours of frantic attempts, they found themselves making no headway. Their focus, energy, and conversation swiftly shifted to a far more critical mission: "What can we do to keep our heads?"

Suddenly, all the screens came back to life, giving them

momentary hope. Those hopes were dashed as the screen displayed a simple message in Russian, "Sosite, Mudaki!," or Suck It Assholes, in English.

Langley. Virginia

Anna Walsh, the CIA's foremost cybersecurity expert, occupied a seat behind a massive monitor within the Director's conference room at CIA headquarters. A mirrored display of her screen was cast on the impressive eighty-five-inch flat screen positioned at the room's forefront. Director Rogers anxiously monitored the scrolling data displayed on the monitor.

Ninety minutes earlier, Sebastian Mitchell had urgently contacted the Director with groundbreaking news. A secure, high-speed satellite link had been hastily established between aiCheckmate's California headquarters and Langley. A wealth of Russian secrets, seemingly electronically pilfered from the Internet Research Agency, scrolled across the room's screen, all while being meticulously recorded on CIA servers.

Bits and bytes flashed across a screen as swiftly as guided missiles aimed at the heart of the Russian state. Cyphers, codes, agent identities, sources, and methods cascaded across the screen. The Director found it challenging to believe in their good fortune. "Can this be the real thing?" asked the Director.

Based on Seb's and Walsh's preliminary assessment, the data appeared to be authentic Russian state secrets of incalculable value. Suddenly, after receiving terabytes of data, the data flow ceased, and an unanticipated message surfaced on the screen, bearing a simple declaration:

"You're welcome. Compliments of Ryan Harman."

A wave of astonishment washed over the room as it fell so silent that you could hear a butterfly flap its wings. Every jaw in the room nearly hit the floor. The Director softly spoke in the hushed room, "Rest In Peace, Mr. Harman... thank you."

St Petersburg - Russia

Traffic was at a standstill on Nevsky Prospect Street outside the luxurious Imperial Towers apartments in the exclusive Nevsky Prospect neighborhood of St. Petersburg. The cause of the jam was a mutilated corpse lying in the road.

Later, Russian Police identified the body of General Novakof, the Director of the Internet Research Agency. An investigation found that he had accidentally fallen from his fourteenth-floor apartment—the victim of a tragic misstep.

Moscow, Russia

In a luxury suite of the Hotel Baltschug Kempinski, Colonel Ivanov of the GRU shared an intimate romantic dinner with his nineteen-year-old, curvaceous, bleach-blond mistress. As they dined on caviar, sipped peppered vodka, and shared a bottle of fine champagne, Inanov's young companion grasped her flute glass with long painted nails. Suddenly, the hotel door burst open with a bang, her hands lost hold of the glass, and it fell to the floor as an uninvited, threatening team of brutish GRU security men barged into the room. The leader of the interlopers rudely barked an order to the Colonel. "Come with us, Ivanov."

"That is Colonel Ivanov to you. Have you forgotten your position?"

"No, not Colonel any longer. From now on, you are a nobody, a fart in the wind." As Ivanov was frog-marched out of the room, his young companion was stricken with a wave of despair. She whispered to herself, "This is a horrifying development. Where will I find another benefactor?"

CHAPTER XXX

PEACE AND UNDERSTANDING

High above the tranquil waters of Deep Water Bay, the team gathered on the covered patio of their safe house, soaking in the panoramic view of the shimmering moonlit sea. Their location, hidden amongst the hills, provided both a strategic security advantage and a serene backdrop for a much-needed respite.

While the calm before the storm is undeniable, it pales in comparison to the peaceful stillness that follows a hurricane. The hurricane had passed for those gathered around the table at the safe house.

With a playful glint in his eye, Ryan gestured to the backyard dining table. "Welcome to our slightly unconventional Last Supper," he grinned. There were no apostles at the patio table. In the place of apostles, he was surrounded by six loyal and formidable mercenaries who had recently proved their mettle.

Ryan's self-deprecating nod to himself as a man returned from the dead brought a few chuckles. At the same time, Dee's recent actions had some playfully comparing her to part-Judas and part-Mary Magdalene, depending on their personal bias.

The grill sizzled as Ryan unveiled massive New York Strip steaks. As he placed a steak on each plate, Jake looked at him and commented, "Is this beef or Brontosaurus?"

The aroma wafted through the air. The steaks were complemented with baked potatoes, and a freshly tossed salad bursting with colors and flavors, drizzled with a simple yet irresistible vinaigrette, and spiced with a hint of minced fresh Thai chilis.

Raising glasses filled with a tasty 2016 Domaine Armand Rousseau Burgundy, Derek offered a toast, "Lady and gentlemen, if

I may have your attention. We faced the unknown with unwavering determination and bravery. We ventured into the heart of danger, and we emerged victorious. Through the darkest of nights, we stood together as a team, a family."

"For duty, honor, and the relentless pursuit of a better world. Cheers!"

"Hear, hear," came the unanimous rejoinder.

Ryan stood, tipped his glass to the assembled diners around the table, and with a deep sense of gratitude, said, "To all of you. Nothing I can say could express my gratitude. I owe you all my life," and overcome by his feelings, he sat down, his voice quivering with emotion.

Everyone at the table took a moment of quiet reflection. Dee leaned over to Ryan and embraced him.

As the moment passed, Kurtz cleared his throat and proposed a toast to Dee, the Russian princess who came through for the entire team, "na zdorov'ye," a Russian toast meaning bless you.

Dee laughed and had a question for Kurtz, "Richard, do you remember when Derek introduced you to Ryan and me? He called you Richard 'Don't-Call-Me-Dick?' What is the story behind that?"

With a soft chuckle, Kurtz responded, "Derek was jerking my chain about an incident from my days in the service. While serving at the Army Garrison Rheinland-Pfalz, Germany, I was tossed in the brig for fighting with my unit's designated ass-hat. You see, me and a few buddies had hall passes, and while out fraulein hunting, we found ourselves at Duffy's Irish Pub, one of our favorite haunts frequented by German ladies looking to hook a GI. I was making progress with a pretty redhead when this asshole, excuse my French, Dee, sabotaged my amorous intentions and interrupted my planned night of love when he said to her, 'Do you know who you're talking to? Meet Dick Kurtz. Who's Dick Hurts, you might ask,.. his Dick Hurts" The ensuing laughter echoed into the night.

Dee tilted her head, curious. "I don't get it."

Ryan helped her out, "You see Dee, Dick is a nickname for Richard, and in addition to a nickname, the word Dick has a male anatomical meaning. When you pair the anatomical Dick with Kurtz's, when you say them together, it takes on a whole different meaning."

Dee shook her head, finally understanding the double entendre.

Eichel, not one to be outdone, recalled his military days when a fellow soldier's questionable music tastes led to a late-night skirmish. He punctuated his story with an exaggerated imitation of the hillbilly, singing, "I've got a humpty dumpty heart, it broke, and it fell apart." leaving everyone in splits.

Derek, always the storyteller, narrated his tale of navigating the intricate maze of Southern family expectations. When he told his long-suffering father, who was married for fifty years to his insufferable mom, my dad cried. "It was the first time I ever saw the old man shed a tear, which shook me up. I mean, he's been married fifty years to my hard-as-nails momma, and his son is getting divorced. Why was he crying? And then it dawned on me... divorce. He didn't know you could do that."

As the night waned and stories flowed, stress from the previous days seemed to evaporate into the night. The camaraderie on display spoke volumes about the bonds forged in the fires of adversity.

As dawn began to paint the horizon, the team dispersed, some seeking the comfort of their beds, others just a quiet corner to reflect. Ryan and Dee retreated to their shared space. Their love, forged in peril and solidified in trust, found a new depth that night.

Amidst the backdrop of impending challenges, the night stood as a hint of hope, laughter, and love ahead for the couple.

The next day was final arrangements day. Derek confirmed that the alternate IDs were ready and in Singapore. Instead of waiting for them in Hong Kong, Ryan and Dee would fly to Singapore to pick up their new identities and spend a few months contemplating what, where, and who they were going to be for the rest of their lives. They would board a private jet ready to take them this evening.

Ryan took Derek aside and said, "Derek, I don't know how much they pay you guys, but it isn't enough. Sentinel hasn't deducted the money from my account yet. It looks like the invoice is for three million eight hundred thousand; here's a signed note from me. I want Sentinel to take an additional three hundred thousand and distribute it to the team. Here's the split: one hundred thousand for you, fifty thousand each for Phil, Kurtz, and Jake, and twenty-five each for the two drivers, Lin and Wong."

Derek said, "You don't have to do that, man. We just did our job, but I will not argue with you."

Ryan replied, "I have one more favor to ask."

Derek heard him out and said. "Count on me."

They shook hands. Ryan pulled Derek closer for a hug and handed him a slip of paper. Derek looked into Ryan's eyes with a serious expression and said, "Harman, if you ever need me, and I hope you never do, I'll be there for you. It was a pleasure serving with you, Sir," and he saluted.

Four hours later, Dee and Ryan were holding hands in a limo heading to the airport. They boarded a private Gulfstream G280 and were on their way to Singapore.

CHAPTER XXXI

MEMORIAL

On a clear winter's day in Washington, DC, The Mayflower Hotel's grand ballroom welcomed about eighty guests, all bound by their connection to Ryan Harman. This grand old lady of Washington hotels, with its enduring elegance and rich history, shimmered under the light of ornate crystal chandeliers, gold-trimmed decor, sumptuous tapestries, and meticulously crafted ceilings, lending the room a gravitas befitting Ryan's memorial.

The service was orchestrated and generously sponsored by aiCheckmate's founder, Sebastian Mitchell. Not only did he ensure all of Ryan's US-based direct reports were present, but Seb also included Raj Patel and Avi Cohen. In a company meeting the previous day, he announced Raj's elevation to the role of CRO, replacing Ryan and Avi's advancement to Sales VP for EMEA and Asia Pac, replacing Raj.

Dominating the room was a poignant photograph of Ryan, his face radiant with a smile. In his arms, his young daughter Phoebe touched his face, her laughter reflecting the pure joy only the innocence of childhood can bring.

With tears streaming down her face, Amy mourned not only for her daughter's loss but also for her late husband, the man she'd shared most of her adult life with. While a part of her felt a bittersweet relief, grateful to be spared the tumultuous battles over assets and custody that come with divorce, she knew this immediate heartache was tougher on her daughter. Yet, she believed in her child's resilience; kids have a remarkable strength to recover and heal.

Avi approached the podium, the strain evident in the reddened bags beneath his bloodshot eyes. "Back when I was a sophomore, my first year of high school, three huge greaser assholes started giving me a hard time. Ryan stepped up and challenged them. They glared at him for a solid ten minutes, but Ryan didn't flinch. He just held their gaze until those bastards threw some choice words our way and backed off. I later asked Ryan if he was really prepared to take on all three of them. He laughed and said, 'Are you shitting me? Any one of those guys would have beaten the crap out of me.' I was puzzled and asked him why he'd stepped in then. He simply said, 'Because you're my friend, and that's what friends do.' That was Ryan for you, always there for a buddy."

A blend of laughter and tears filled the room as many recognized the essence of Ryan in Avi's story.

Carla Pushkin stepped up to the podium, her gaze meeting Phoebe's. "Phoebe," she began gently, "I have a son. And when he grows up, if he becomes even half the man your father was, I'd be immensely proud. Your dad was the epitome of a true gentleman. He had the most beautiful and honest heart. He treated everyone, be it a man or woman, CEO or a busboy, with respect. He taught me so much, and I often wish I could've repaid his kindness. Whenever he spoke of you his face would shine with love and pride. I genuinely ache for your loss. But always remember, every one of us, everyone who worked with your dad, we're all here for you. We're your extended family, now and always." With that, Carla approached Amy, planting a gentle kiss on her cheek before wrapping the grief-stricken Phoebe in a warm, comforting embrace.

Raj, donning his Tartan kilt, took his place at the podium. He recounted his first encounter with Ryan. Knowing Ryan was in search of a UK salesperson and was at the Paddington Hilton in London, he reached out. "So I ring him up, and he goes, 'Aye, I'm needin' a salesman,'" Raj said in his thick Scottish brogue. "And I retort, 'Nae, ye're lookin' for a global sales VP.' To which he firmly replies, 'Nay, I'm not.'" Raj paused, letting out a chuckle. "So I tell him we're meetin' noon, right there in the executive lounge of the hotel. Over a few hearty pints and some stilton cheese, we get to chattin', and he finally admits, 'Aye, ye're right. I'm in need of a Global Sales VP. When can ye start?'"

Raj's eyes twinkled as he continued, "Ryan, he was a decisive bloke, yet could bend when need be. I've had me best moments with that lad. And, if ye can even fathom, some of the loudest laughs too. So here's to Ryan Harman. To our departed mate, a leader and comrade, your mark remains unmatched in our midst. Even though ye've left us, in our tales and hearts, your wisdom and spirit remain everlasting."

Dex, the former Marine, currently aiCheckmate's New England sales exec, solemnly stood in the back of the room. He'd buried more than a few comrades in his career in the Corps. This was his first civilian casualty. He listened intently to his colleagues, who were lucky enough to have many years of experience with Harman, reminiscing about Ryan's effect on their lives. Although Dex had known Ryan for just a few years, a bond of mutual respect and trust had quickly formed. He had hoped to grow that bond and learn from the man over many more years. That was not to be.

Sentinel's Derek Garner sat silently next to Dex. He knew Dex through a mutual friend, Roger "the Dodger." His presence was twofold. He was there to pay respects to a man he admired and to fulfill an oath. Derek was on a mission. Standing respectfully at the back of the room, he thought to himself, "I'm the only person here who knows that we're paying our respects to a living man."

CHAPTER XXXII

PHOEBE

Washington, DC

As the memorial concluded, Derek approached Avi. "May I have a moment of your time, privately?"

Avi raised his eyebrows, furrowed his brow, and inquired, "Who are you?"

"My name is Derek Garner; I was the leader of Ryan's protection team."

"Well, you fucked that up, didn't you," Avi replied scornfully. "I'm surprised you had the balls to show your face here after screwing the pooch like you did."

Holding back his anger, Derek understood the pain Avi was feeling. He forgave Avi's uninformed disrespect. If any other person on any other day talked smack to Derek like that, they would have been carried out on a stretcher. Derek held back his rage, kept his temper in check, and replied. "I understand you feeling that way, and yes, I failed. That is a guilt I will take to my grave. I had nothing but the utmost respect for your good friend. Days before we lost him, he gave me a note and told me that if anything should happen to him, I was to find you and give you this." He handed Avi an envelope and said, "I know that there are no words that can make up for my failure and your loss. I'm sorry." Derek turned and silently walked away.

Avi hurried to his room, sat at the hotel desk, and opened the letter. It read:

> *"Avi, if you're reading this, I'm gone. You've been more than a friend to me... much more. I have a final*

request. Enclosed are bank account details. I've set aside five million dollars for Phoebe's future. Please oversee this fund, help it grow, and give her control of the account on Phoebe's twenty-fifth birthday. Tell her I put this aside for her and counsel her to manage it wisely. I trust no one more than you with this task. I'm sorry to burden you, but I know I can count on you to honor my last wish. I love you, my brother."

The debilitating sadness of the last week, and now this added responsibility, weighed heavily on him. He realized he would never see Ryan again and how much he would miss his friend of so many years. Then he thought of Phoebe and the pain she was suffering. Avi, who had experienced war and lost comrades, knew the pain of personal loss and was heartbroken. He looked at the note, a tear dropping on the paper, and then he stopped holding back, put his head in his hands, and wept uncontrollably.

Eight Years Later - Maryland

Eight years transformed Ryan's little girl, Phoebe, into a radiant, intellectually gifted, graceful young woman. After graduating from the tony Holton Arms School in Bethesda, Maryland, she felt ready to leave her provincial life in the Washington D.C. suburbs and take on the world. Her social calendar was bustling, filled with gatherings of friends and the occasional interested suitor. As a testament to her academic prowess, she graduated as one of Holton's top five students. She was active in extracurricular activities and shone as a violinist in the school's orchestra. She was the number one ranked singles player on Holton's state championship tennis team.

Summer after graduation, Uncle Avi invited Phoebe to spend a pre-university summer with him and his family in Israel. Her mom had other ideas, but Phoebe persuaded Amy to let her go. Strong-headed like her dad, Phoebe was not to be denied. Accompanied by her closest confidante, Sophie, the two planned to spend their time soaking up the sun and the culture.

Israel

Avi and his wife Tali coddled the two girls and acted as tour guides, armed guards, chaperones, and interpreters. The Cohens arranged travel throughout the country, offering the girls a view of the real Israel. Avi regaled Phoebe with tales of Ryan speaking in awe of him as if he were Ulysses on some mythic Greek quest. He spoke of Ryan's love of the Israeli beaches and how they would swim in the warm, azure-blue Mediterranean waters. They'd body surf till they washed up on the beach like exhausted rag dolls. Avi told her that once, after a long day at the beach, her Dad said, "Avi, someday, when I retire, I will find a quiet, pretty beach town in a quiet little corner of the world, and I'll open some kind of shop. I'll slow down, breathe the air, and live the beachcomber life." And then he added, "I like to think of your dad on a beach somewhere in heaven."

Through Avi's tales, Phoebe gained a newfound appreciation for her father. Seeing her father through Avi's eyes and heart made her proud and saddened her simultaneously.

New York City

By mid-August, Phoebe was back home, bustling with preparations for her inaugural year at Columbia University. In New York, her adopted Aunt Carla Pushkin welcomed Phoebe as an integral part of her family, and Phoebe was a frequent guest at Carla's Eighty-second Street, Park Avenue West, brownstone home. Carla recently completed her graduate studies at Columbia and was now a practicing psychologist with an office in the basement of her home.

The Pushkin family warmly embraced Phoebe. Carla, or "Aunt" Carla as Phoebe fondly called her, offered insights that deepened Phoebe's understanding of the reverence her father commanded among his peers and friends.

Carla reminisced about Ryan's passion for travel, especially his fondness for the world's most beautiful beaches. Inspired by his vivid descriptions of his travels, Carla, alongside her husband Mark and their two sons, once took a two-week vacation to the Great Barrier Reef. "Your dad had it spot on," Carla remarked.

In Phoebe's senior year, she applied for and was awarded a Rhodes Scholarship. She looked forward to this next chapter of her life in England.

Oxford, United Kingdom

Uncle Raj would frequently visit Phoebe while she studied for her MS in Neuroscience at Oxford. Here was another occasion for her to realize her father's profound effect on the lives of those who knew and loved him.

Raj was a comical character to Phoebe. She especially loved his bigger-than-life swagger, his talent for storytelling, his humor, and most of all, his Scottish brogue, which at times required a translator to turn his phrases that were allegedly the king's English into a language that an American could comprehend.

Raj's language difficulties were highlighted in one of his favorite stories. "Let me tell you about the time your da took me to his hometown for pizza, at Tony's, a bloody dive in a dingy strip mall in a shire named after Mr. Thomas Alva Edison."

Raj exclaimed, "Ach, the place was a wee bit of a dive, with dreary linoleum booth tables and bench seats, lined with well-worn pleather, it was. But then, lassie, there's the pizza. The crust's right bonnie thin and crisp, givin' ye that satisfyin' crunch with each bite. The sauce, sweet but no' too much, marries the cheese topping just perfectly. I cannae blame yer da for loving this joint." And ya da says to me, "There is no better pizza than Tony's."

"So, we've finished our grub, and this auld lassie in a black waitress outfit, her gray locks tied up in a bun, says, 'Use guys done dare,' and I glance at yer da and ask your da, 'Whit did she just say?' And yer da replies, 'That's Jersey for 'Have you fine gentleman finished dining with us this fine evening?'"

Your da was a Jersey boy in his heart. And lassie? He was a great man. Funny, warm, smart, and loyal… an' I loved him."

"I learn more about him from you and his friends every time we meet. I'm sorry that I never really had a chance to know him as anything but the father of me as a little girl," replied Phoebe.

On the dawn of Phoebe's 25th birthday, her phone buzzed to life. The incoming call displayed the name of Avi, Uncle Avi, her father's closest friend. She loved Avi. She loved all her father's people, but Avi, Phoebe thought, if this was Oz, and I was Dorothy, Avi would be my scarecrow. Uncle Avi, with his protective demeanor and warm nature, had been a constant in her life since Ryan's passing. "Happy birthday, Phoebe!" Avi's voice boomed with its usual enthusiasm. He mentioned he was in the UK for a meeting with Raj in London but wanted to take some time to celebrate her special day.

With the sun hanging high and the streets of Oxford bustling with activity, they decided to meet at The Grand Café on High Street. The café, reputed to be the first coffee house in England, was charming with its ornate ceilings and marble tables. Sunlight streamed through the tall windows, reflecting off silverware and china, casting a golden hue over everything.

The menu boasted a range of English breakfasts, artisan sandwiches, and fresh pastries. Phoebe, with a penchant for savory, chose the smoked salmon bagel with cream cheese, capers, and red onion. Avi, always with an appetite, went for the full English breakfast – eggs, sausage, bacon, mushrooms, and tomatoes, paired with a steaming cup of black coffee.

As they ate and reminisced, Avi's demeanor turned serious. He slid a neatly folded piece of paper across the table. It was a bank statement from an account in the Cayman Islands. Phoebe's eyes widened as she scanned the digits, the balance just shy of twelve and a half million dollars.

"Before your father passed," Avi began, his voice heavy with emotion, "he entrusted me with this. He wanted to ensure your future was secure. He asked me to manage it and, on your twenty-fifth birthday, to hand it over to you."

Phoebe's eyes shimmered with tears. "But why didn't you tell me before?"

Avi sighed, "He wanted you to grow up without the weight of this responsibility. He wanted you to find your path without the shadow of immense wealth. He trusted me to grow the fund, and I've tried my best."

The weight of the moment settled between them. Phoebe grappled with a whirlwind of emotions – gratitude for her father's foresight, the staggering reality of her newfound wealth, and a profound respect for Avi, who had honored her father's wishes to the letter.

"I miss him, Avi. If only I had the chance to know him better," she whispered.

EPILOGUE

"It's always better to sacrifice your opponent's men."
— *Savielly Tartakower*

AFTER THE END

In the picturesque shire of Noosa, located in Queensland, Australia, lies the sun-kissed beach town of Noosa Heads. Among the myriad cafes, boutiques, and beachfront establishments is a standout surf shop named "Hang Ten Down Under." Owned and lovingly managed by Gary and Natalia Hart, this shop has become a cornerstone of the community.

Gary and Natalia are not just business partners but soulmates whose love story is as captivating as the waves of Noosa. They came to Noosa Heads a dozen years earlier. You'd find them stealing glances at each other across the shop or sharing an inside joke, their laughter echoing through the aisles. Their love story wasn't just limited to the confines of their shop; they are often seen hand in hand on the beach, watching the sunset or participating in community beach clean-ups. Every summer, they organize a surfing competition for the local youngsters, promoting both sport and community.

The interior of "Hang Ten Down Under" mirrors the vibrant and warm spirit of the couple. The wooden floors, bleached by the sun, are covered in colorful, intricate patterns of surfboard fins and ocean waves. Surfboards of all sizes and designs line the walls, with each board having a unique story that Gary or Natalia would eagerly share. The shop also boasts a wide range of surf gear - from wetsuits to sunglasses and even artisanal beach jewelry crafted by local artists.

In one corner is a cozy lounge area with bean bags and a small collection of books. This is where locals and tourists alike often find themselves engrossed in surfing tales or sharing their own ocean adventures.

Natalia, with her keen eye for detail, manages the apparel section. It's a vibrant collection of comfortable and sustainable surf clothing, drawing inspiration from indigenous art and Australia's rich coastal culture.

Gary, on the other hand, is the surfboard expert. Passionate and knowledgeable, he's always ready to give advice or share a surfing tip, ensuring that everyone, from beginners to pros, finds their perfect board.

Together, the Harts have made "Hang Ten Down Under" more than just a shop; it's a hub for the community, a testament to their love for each other, and their shared passion for their neighbors.

One particular morning, as the sun's golden rays stretched out, Gary left his beachfront home to open the shop. Choosing the scenic beach route, he walked on the soft, cool sand, indulging in the rhythmic lullaby of the waves and the invigorating sea breeze. However, unbeknownst to him, a young woman trailed a short distance behind, her observant eyes fixated on him.

Suddenly, a prickling sensation at the back of his neck made Gary acutely aware of his surroundings. He turned to find an attractive young woman, her blonde curly hair gleaming in the sun and her piercing blue eyes staring directly at him. There was an overwhelming familiarity in those eyes.

"Dad?" she whispered a quiver in her voice.

A torrent of emotions swelled within Gary... no, Ryan. The weight of twenty years of secrets, of hiding, of suppressed pain from leaving behind the one he cherished most in the world crashed heavily down upon him like a ten-ton weight. Phoebe, his precious daughter, stood before him. The very thought of never seeing her again had been a constant ache in his heart, yet here she was, as real as the sand beneath his feet.

Phoebe's eyes welled up, mirroring the storm of emotions churning inside her. For years, she had grappled with grief, believing her father was dead. Yet, the stories shared with her by those who loved her father kept him alive, if only in her mind. His body was never found; she started thinking, what if? And designated a significant portion of her newfound wealth to discover her "what if."

"Daddy," she choked out, stepping closer, and just started sobbing uncontrollably.

Ryan, eyes shining with tears, said, "Phoebe, oh my girl, you don't know how hard this has been. My love for you and my desire to keep you safe caused both of us so much pain. It was to keep your heart beating that I broke your heart."

She nodded, her earlier investigations having revealed some of the dangers her father had faced. "I understand, Dad. I've spent years trying to piece everything together to find you. I needed to see you, know the truth, and tell you that I love you no matter what."

Ryan reached out, pulling Phoebe into a tight embrace. The past and present converged in that heartfelt moment on the beach, two souls reuniting against all odds, enveloped by the love and understanding that had never truly waned.

THE END

ABOUT THE AUTHOR

Glen Hellman

Glen Hellman's career began in 1978 when he joined an early-stage technology startup. Since then, he has been a pivotal member of numerous startup teams, contributing in roles spanning sales, marketing, and product management. He has also served as a senior executive, board member, and investor.

Today, Hellman is a distinguished faculty member at the University of Maryland. He instructs Ph.D. researchers from a plethora of esteemed institutions, including Carnegie Mellon, Penn State, University of Pennsylvania, Johns Hopkins, University of Maryland, Howard University, George Washington University, Virginia Tech, Hampton University, University of North Carolina, and NC State. His teachings are part of a National Science Foundation program that aims to transform innovative technology from federally funded university labs into commercial applications.

Beyond academia, Hellman is a sought-after executive leadership coach. He collaborates with CEOs and executive leadership teams, either in one-on-one sessions or peer groups. His primary objective is to guide these leaders in discerning their next steps and ensuring they take decisive actions.

"Cyphers & Sighs" marks Hellman's debut in fiction. He has also penned the non-fiction title, "Intentional Leadership," a definitive guide for leaders aiming to cultivate trust and confidence while building and leading high-performance teams. The book is available on Amazon.

For more information about Glen Hellman, visit:

http://www.cxoelevate.com

Made in the USA
Middletown, DE
12 November 2023